Cabaret Island 1956

Mystery on the Mississippi River

JUDY LEWIN

Copyright © 2015 by Judy Lewin
Cover Design Art by Create Space
All Rights reserved.
Published in the United States by Lunna Investments
Saint Louis, Missouri
ISBN-10: 099045391X
ISBN-13: 978-0990453918

1. Cabaret Island 1956 (Carol Burke – Fictitious character) – Fiction. 2. Romance – Historical. 3. Mystery – Historical.
4. Midwest – Mississippi River.

1 River men Tug

Carol Burke sat at her ancient desk in the clubhouse of the Cabaret Boat Dock, north of St. Louis on the Mississippi River. A battered, white yacht cap tilted far back on her curly auburn brown, close-cropped hair. Her snug turtleneck sweater enhanced the curves of her firm, full bosom and a pair of tight-fitting faded blue short shorts accented her well-rounded hips. She crushed her cigarette in a tin ashtray and glanced in hostile silence at a burly Frank Weaver plopped in an oak captain's chair beside her.

"Okay. I can't pay you," she said. "What do you want me to do? You tell me." Her low, throaty voice had a sharp edge.

"You've got to pay something before long." Frank rose and leaned his left shoulder forward to make a fist. He jerked his thumb's pad at her, and then pushed his arm forward three times to hammer the point. "You've got to make a mortgage payment. Anything," he said. Already bald and chubby at thirty-two years of age, Frank reveled in dominating Carol.

"It's easy for you to say that," she said. "I'm doing the best I can. As soon as I get some cash, I'll pay you. What more do you expect?"

Frank changed his tone. "Think real hard, Carol Jean." Everyone along the river knew her by this name. A cautious smile curled the corners of his mouth and his eyelids lowered.

"I am thinking. You're making me a proposition," she snapped.

"I didn't say that," he replied.

"You sure tried to look it!"

His eyes narrowed again. "I can make things pretty tough for you."

"You can't make them any tougher than they already are."

"We could take this place over." Frank's bank represented the Ebbs Estate, a St. Louis trustee that held the mortgage.

"Do that, and you'd play hell getting your money for sure."

Carol glared a bitter look, and then shrugged. The Cabaret Boat Dock and Club House had been inherited from her father, a retired Mississippi River pilot, and still mortgaged to the hilt. It had been a time when women could not buy property or open a bank checking account in their own name. Business had dropped to almost nothing in 1952 after Route 66 was widened to four lanes and the Chain of Rocks Bridge deserted. Car traffic no longer ferried from Granite City, Illinois to St. Louis. This year, President Eisenhower had signed the Interstate Highway Act of 1956, so she felt like the world was passing her by.

Carol felt completely alone. She grabbed hold of the Iroquois talisman spirit in Manitou stone on her desk that held the memory of a powerful dream and her now deceased mother's energy to give her strength.

"You don't want us to foreclose and neither do I, Carol Jean," Frank went on. He lowered his voice to almost a whisper. "Think it over."

"You still haven't said what you want me to do," said Carol.

"Do I have to draw you a picture?"

"Then it is a proposition."

"I love you, Carol," Frank said in a nostalgic voice. "It doesn't have to be a proposition. You know that. Just breathe the word, and I'd find the nearest minister." Frank gazed at her, hope flaming in his black eyes.

Carol froze a contemptuous glare back. Frank chuckled. "That's what I figured. Well, you can't blame me for trying, kid," he said. "When a guy is crazy about a girl like I am about you, he'll do anything."

Frank's tone changed, now thick with emotion. "I dream about you all the time. About holding you, kissing you. I go crazy inside of me. That's why I've got to proposition you, as you call it. That's my story, Carol. What do you say?"

She told him. Her blunt language caused Frank's face to turn dark crimson. When she finished, his mouth worked without making a sound and his eyes were mere slits.

"Get out of here!" she ordered.

"I'll be back, don't worry. One word from me and the trustees of the estate will attach everything you own."

"Go ahead have them do that. They'll lose too, and miss out on getting publicity to conserve wildlife on Cabaret Island. So you won't look so good either when I tell them their administrator has been trying to collect something besides their money."

Carol stood up. She had had enough of Frank Weaver for the afternoon. It was not the first time he had harassed her for a debt payment, or a free evening in lieu thereof. One of these days he would call her bluff. Her only hope was that she could get through the summer season. After that she dreaded to think what might happen.

Carol picked up a pair of binoculars as she left the clubhouse. Frank followed her out. His frustration became even more agonizing as he saw the golden sheen cast by the late afternoon sun on her smooth legs. Grimly he got into his car and drove back to Riverview Drive.

She watched him leave, thinking that Frank would be her only trouble. She raised the eight-power lenses. Looking south toward St. Louis City, she surveyed the broad bend of the Mississippi River until she located a sand dredge with a tugboat at its stern. The dredge's headlights were out of the water, and the tug was churning up a wake. Carol felt relief.

Joe Mosley is the tug's skipper and had orders to move the dredge. For a month he had been working just south of the Cabaret Boat Dock and had made the clubhouse his headquarters. He had become as much of a nuisance to Carol as Frank Weaver, except in a different way. He treated her like his private property. She hoped he would get ordered to New Orleans or St. Paul.

Just before she lowered the glasses, she glimpsed an unfamiliar sight in the channel to the right of the dredge – a trim, white cabin cruiser working its way up the river. She studied it a moment without recognition.

"We might have a new customer tonight, Matt," she remarked.

As Matt Davenport painted the Cabaret Island ship's lantern, he looked up. An elderly, gray-haired man who worked around the clubhouse and dock, his eyes squinted down river.

"Is Mr. Mosley on his way up, Cap'n?" Matt had called Carol Jean *Cap'n* ever since she was a kid and made her feel in charge.

"No. I don't think I'll have to bother with him tonight, for a change. But there is a cruiser headed this way."

"It'll probably pass us by to go to the Alton Lake," Matt predicted with pessimism.

"It might stop here for some gas. You'd better go down and move the skiff away from the pump just in case," she said in reference to a small flat bottom boat.

Matt descended the rickety stairs to the L-shaped dock that floated on the murky current below the river bank. Two slips had canopy protection overhead.

Carol turned back to the clubhouse, a low, wooden building, framed by two large elm trees on the river bank. Inside, a small lunch counter overlooked the river. At the opposite end of the room, there were shelves and bins, containing rope, shackles, boat spikes and a conglomeration of marine hardware that Carol sold to the few remaining yachtsmen on this stretch of the river. Her desk sat in a private corner, surrounded with ledgers, copies of the mortgage, and a locked metal box with love letters addressed to her mother from her father. She made her living quarters in the rear.

Carol sat down at her desk and spent half an hour going over her accounts. She had run up quite a few charges in getting ready for the season. No matter how she figured, she was still far in the red. Only a miracle could save her from bankruptcy. She passed her tired hand across her pretty forehead.

"That boat is putting in, Cap'n," Matt called out to her.

Carol looked up. The cabin cruiser that she had seen through the binoculars edged into the dock. It was a trim craft, some thirty feet long with a nine-foot beam. Its name *HADLEY* was lettered in gold across the square-cut stern and repeated in smaller letters below the forward window of the deckhouse. Matt went down, and a young man in a T-shirt passed him a line to hitch to a vertical pole above the gasoline pump.

Carol left her desk and went to the dock – swaying gently from the wash of the cruiser. The young man's eyes swept up her supple legs, the luscious curves of her sweater and came to rest, with surprise and pleasure, on her attractive, soft rounded face.

"Hello," he smiled. He had a lean and athletic build, not quite six feet tall. His dark hair was cut short, and his deep-brown eyes had an interested twinkle.

"I don't remember seeing this boat before. Where're you from?"

"Cincinnati. Monte Abbott is my name." He found it difficult to remove his eyes from the sun tanned, well built brunette.

"You want some gas, I suppose, "she said. "Matt will take care of you." She wondered if he was headed north to Alton Lake.

"Yes, and I want to dock here if you've got room for me. What do you charge?"

"For a boat this size it'll be ten dollars a week. How long will you be here?"

"I don't know. A few days, a few weeks, maybe all summer," he grinned.

Carol smiled. This would be a break, to get a new customer. "You'll find the dock convenient."

"I know that. A fellow in Paducah recommended this place."

"Who?" she asked.

"A tugboat captain by the name of George Anderson."

"Oh yeah. My dad and he were friends for years."

Carol had been well known on the river since her birth in 1933, not only because she was Sam Burke's daughter, but because she blossomed into a smart and intriguing beauty too. Her good looks attracted any leftover business for the Cabaret Boat Dock and its ramshackle shore establishment.

Monte Abbott glanced toward the clubhouse. "Can I get something to eat up there? I want to make a phone call too."

"Our cook has the night off, but I can fix you something. Come along," she said.

Monte chewed on his lower lip as he followed her up the wooden steps. His eyes were level with her well rounded calves. He became fascinated.

In the clubhouse she pointed to a telephone booth. While he made his phone call, Carol went behind the counter and put two pork chops on the grill. She had decided to fix her own dinner while she was at it.

The young man stayed in the booth for twenty minutes. When he came out, he had a troubled look was on his face. For a moment, he just stared into space - as if something had distracted him. All at once he glanced at Carol cooking at the grill.

"Do you serve drinks here? I've got some liquor on my boat, but I'd like to buy—"

"We don't sell it, but you're welcome to what I've got." She turned and set a bottle of bourbon on the counter-top.

"Have one with me. Please."

Carol hesitated. She did not make a habit of drinking with customers, unless she knew them pretty well. Since there was no one else in the clubhouse and Frank Weaver's visit had worn on her nerves, she needed something to life her spirits.

"Don't mind if I do," she said. "But you can't pay for it. I don't have a liquor license."

She made two highballs. After she took a sip, she studied him again. He wore polished oxford loafers and khaki slacks – looked as if he had little to do. You had to be that way to own an expensive boat and then use it for pleasure. He was not a river man – something in his favor. Carol felt river men were just a bunch of tomcats.

"Are you having trouble getting someone to come after you?" She asked thinking the phone call made him unhappy.

"No as things have turned out, I'll dock here tonight and sleep aboard the *Hadley*." He emptied his glass and it wasn't hard to see that he wanted another drink. She offered him one.

"Would you mind?" he asked.

"Help yourself."

"He didn't stop with just more highball. Carol didn't keep track, but he took three more in a short space of time. When his dinner was ready, she set a plate of food on a table.

Monte Abbott got off the stool. He staggered over to the table and sat down. Halfway through his meal he noticed Carol eating behind the lunch counter. He asked her to join him. She hesitated a moment, then complied. She picked up her plate with a pork chop and vegetables, poured herself a cup of coffee and carried it to the table.

"Isn't it unusual for a woman to run a dock?" he asked when she sat down.

"I'm the only woman in this business that I know of." Briefly she explained how it had come about. "I should have sold out when my Dad died."

"You seem to be doing okay."

"No. Running a dock is a man's job. Besides, all the business moved up to Alton Lake. That's where the boating is. It started after the Corp of Civil Engineers completed the Alton dam, but Dad couldn't see it. He kept saying it was too far from St Louis, and he was right – until the highway Route 66 was built. It doesn't take long to drive up there now.

"That's too bad," he said with sympathy.

"There's still a small profit left in the launch. I ferry people across to Cabaret Island to picnic and swim and observe the wildlife. I'm in the local Sierra Club to prevent Las Vegas investors from converting the island into a gambling bonanza."

"I'd think it would be fun to run a dock," Monte speculated. "I'm crazy about boats and the river. I guess that's my trouble."

"I love the river, too. It's always been my home. I was born on a steamboat, just north of Cape Girardeau," she said, thinking about her birth place in the "River City."

Her extraordinary, luminous blue-green eyes grew distant for a moment. She had never known a normal childhood. Her backyard had been the stern deck of a tugboat. Her playmates had been river pilots, engineers and roustabouts. She had gotten her education in snatches, in the winter-time at Cairo, Chester and Hannibal. If she seemed older than her twenty-four years, it was because she was a realist when it came to money, men and the Mississippi River.

She found it pleasant and relaxing, sitting here in the twilight with this good looking young man. There was an air of refinement about him which was a refreshing change for her. Maybe it was his education. She didn't know. She had noticed it in some of the other men who owned pleasure boats. There were tomcats among them, too, but not the alley variety. They were not rough like Joe Mosley and other river men she knew.

For the first time that day she forgot her troubles in Monte's company. They were still sitting at the table, visiting, when a car turned off of Riverview drive. Its headlights came around the curving road to the clubhouse and stopped. A moment later the screen door opened and Joe Mosley swaggered in.

"Hi, gorgeous," he called to her. Joe's big grin gave way to a scowl when he caught sight of Monte.

Joe had a powerful young man's build, with dark and curly hair. His heavy jaw, thick neck and bulging muscles gave him the appearance of a wrestler. He wore a light jacket and a steamboat cap.

Carol introduced the two men. "Joe is skipper of the tug, the *Della Darby*," she said for Monte's benefit.

"Glad to know you," Monte said as he stood up and shook hands. Joe said nothing.

"Mr. Abbott came in on a cruiser from Cincinnati," Carol explained.

Joe eyed Monte without favor and sat down. He gave his full attention to Carol as he spoke. 'We're moving the dredge down to a spot near the Meramec River. Got a job there that will take about a week."

"I noticed you were up to something this afternoon," she said.

Monte sat at the table with them as they talked, but he did not intrude on their conversation. Joe could stay only a few minutes. He had to get back on the job. He wanted to let Carol know where he would be, in case she needed him for anything.

"Maybe I can help her look after things," said Monte as Joe rose to go. "It looks like I'm going to be around for a while." He said with a good natured and friendly smile.

Joe gazed at Monte with a hard face and unpleasant glint in his eyes. "Look, mister," Joe said. "You're a customer of Carol's and that's just fine." A note of warning crept into his voice. "So take my advice and keep it that way. Nobody bothers this gal, not if I know about it."

Carol glared at Joe. He had no right to talk that way in front of a customer, but before she could take him to task he went out. It was probably just as well. She would have turned on Joe and might have given Monte Abbott the wrong idea about her.

2 Phone Call after midnight

Monte showed no concern over Joe Moseley's ominous advice. He was talking of other things before the tail lights of Joe's car disappeared onto Riverview Drive. Finally, Monte stood up. "I need to get my boat squared away. How much do I owe you for dinner tonight, Carol?" he asked.

'I oughtn't to charge you anything. It wasn't a regular meal."

"Nonsense." He tossed a five-dollar bill on the table. "That includes the water I drank with the whiskey."

"I'd better go with you. It's hard to find the slip at night where you'll moor the boat," she said.

The night air had cooled, and the weather was balmy. The distant lights from St. Louis made a soft, rosy glow in the sky. To the north, the twinkling lights of the water works plant reflected in the dark current of the river. Matt had turned on a dock light earlier in the evening. Carol could have made her way in pitch darkness. She knew every inch of the way. But Monte stumbled twice, and then caught himself. He was not only a stranger to the dock, but unsteady from the drinks.

"I'd better steer the boat around for you," she suggested, realizing his condition.

"I appreciate that."

She unfastened the lead cable line and walked back to the boat. Monte helped her aboard, though she was steadier than he. His hand on her bare arm sparked a pleasant shiver. In the cockpit, he started the motor for her, and then stepped aside so she could take the wheel.

"Turn your running lights on," she said.

"Aye, skipper," he smiled.

Carol allowed the current to carry the boat downstream. When it fell astern of the dock, she put the motor in forward speed, but kept it slow. As they gathered headway, she turned the stern of the boat toward shore and brought it at a snail's pace between the dock and the river bank. She cut the motor just before they nosed into the slip she had assigned to the *Hadley*. They put out a line from the stern to the dock's post as an added precaution against the vagrancies of the current.

"You handle this boat like you've been doing it all your life," Monte said as he turned on an overhead light in the deckhouse.

"What do you expect of a river girl?" she said, tilting her head at him and smiling.

"Would you like to look around while you're aboard?" he asked.

She nodded. He showed her to the forward sleeping quarters. Carol was impressed with the neatness it showed after such a long trip. The galley just ahead of the deckhouse was equally ship-shape. While she stood in the galley admiring the atmosphere, he suggested a nightcap.

"You've had enough to drink, haven't you?" Carol eyed him with amusement.

"No, I had too many on an empty stomach."

Quickly he mixed some drinks and carried them out to the stern. They sat down. A billion stars twinkled low in the sky as Carol leaned back against the cushion of the deck seat.

"Are you in the habit of cruising from Cincinnati by yourself every so often?" she asked.

"This is my longest trip, but I've been up and down the Ohio many times. But then, this isn't a pleasure trip."

"Coming by river is a slow way to get here on business."

"I needed some time to think through a problem and the *Hadley* is the best place I know for that." He studied his drink in silence for a minute, and then asked, "Why is it that some people don't like boats?"

She smiled. "Well, I guess for the same reason some don't like horses, or trains. I wish more people liked them. I could sure use the business."

"Take a girl like you," Monte went on. "You've been around boats all your life. Now I could understand if you got tired of being around them. It's more of a job to you. But I can't see why any other girl wouldn't enjoy a cruise now and then."

"Frankly, I don't either," she agreed.

"Would you take a cruise with me sometime?" he asked without warning. "I'd like to go up through the lock of that dam at Alton lake."

"This is the first time I've even been invited to take a cruise – for the purpose of seeing the Alton Pool." she exclaimed.

At first Monte did not understand. Then he got her meaning. A deliberate smile crossed his face. "I'm a knucklehead. You see how daffy a guy can get about boats. But wouldn't it be fun to go up there sometime?"

Carol thought it would, but did not say so. She had been on cabin cruises with young men who had a lot less going for them than Monte Abbot.

"It's hard for me to get away from the dock, especially with the season getting under way," she replied.

"But would you, Carol?" there was a boyish eagerness in his voice.

"We'll see about that. You can get up there and back in a day easily."

"I'm going to hold you to that." He sounded quite sincere.

He reached for her empty glass and his arm brushed her bare leg – Carol's nerves tingled. It felt like limbs waking from a long sleep needing to flex, to come alive.

"Don't fix another for me, Monte. I've got to get back to the clubhouse," she said.

There was too much excitement in his nearness. She liked it, but did not trust it. She had known him less than four hours. This was no way to start out with a new customer.

"Please have one more with me," he begged. "I'll make it light."

Before she could protest, he went to the galley. Disturbing warmth filled her. Monte Abbott's arrival at the Cabaret Dock had brought a much needed change. She had grown tired of Joe Mosley and his rough possessiveness – she was weary of her financial troubles. She had to be careful, very careful, not to let herself get out of hand tonight.

When Monte came back with the drinks she concentrated on keeping a safe distance from him. He turned off the light in the deckhouse, lit two cigarettes and gave her one. The tips glowing red in the darkness. His voice was quiet, drawing her closer.

"I was lucky to tie up at your dock," he told her.

"There aren't many to choose from this close to St Louis," she said, trying to keep the conversation down-to-earth, worrying about his romantic undertone.

"If I had gone to one of the others, I wouldn't have met you," said Monte, looking at her in the darkness.

She felt his eyes on her. This would never do. She emptied her glass and flipped her cigarette away. It made a thin red arc over the side of the boat and vanished as it touched the water.

"I've got to get back," she said, standing up.

Monte stood beside her. His hands pulled her to him. She looked up. It seemed the most natural thing in the world having his lips pressed against hers. She was amazed at the strength in his slender body. Carol made no effort to pull away. For a long moment, she let him hold her, enjoying the pleasure of his embrace and returned his eager caress. Next, she pushed him away. She had to stop now, or not at all.

"See you in the morning," she said. Her voice choked.

"It's been wonderful with you, Carol. Good night."

She stepped to the dock, calling good night as she hurried away. At the end of the ramp she paused to pull an electric switch that turned off the dock lights, except for those required for navigation. Then she ran up the steps.

Ten minutes later, she closed the clubhouse for the night and retreated to the other room. Its walls were covered with pictures of steamboats, tugs, and river personalities—mementoes of her father's lifetime on the river. Carol had kept them undisturbed. The room had three easy chairs and a table; in one corner a large double bed. A dressing table supplied the only feminine touch: a photo of her mother dated 1935 and a small closet contained her clothes.

Carol changed into a pair of summer weight pajamas. Before getting into bed, she stood in the darkness by the window, looking toward the river. A sultry breeze came through. She thought of the young man on his cruiser below the river bank. She knew he came from Cincinnati, had made a phone call, and then drank a lot. She knew nothing else. She wondered what worried him.

Sleep came slow as she lay on her bed. She turned from side to side, not able to calm down. At last she lay on her back, legs and arms outstretched. A peaceful relaxation gradually came over her. The ringing of the telephone in the clubhouse jarred her awake.

Carol was petulant. *All right, all right, hold everything. I'm coming.* Still half asleep, she went to the phone booth and picked up the receiver.

"Hello."

"Is this the Cabaret Dock or something like that?" asked an unyielding, feminine voice.

"Yes."

"Let me speak to Mr. Abbott," the voice commanded.

"He's settled in on his boat."

"Well go get him."

The caller issued the order with such arrogance that Carol stood stunned for a moment. She was not accustomed to taking orders, and was irked by the haughty tone.

"Did you hear what I said?" the voice demanded.

"Yes, I heard you," Carol said between her teeth.

"Well?"

Carol managed to keep control. "It'll take a few minutes. Would you care to leave your number? I'll tell him to call you back."

"Listen, I haven't got all night. Go get him right now," the voice shouted.

Carol's lips compressed tight as she lowered the receiver to dangle on its cord. She fought off an impulse to give the woman on the other end a sample of colorful river curse words, but instead marched out of the clubhouse, seething. She went halfway down to the dock before she realized she still wore her flimsy pajamas. Carol stopped.

On second thought, she went on. It was dark. No one was around, in this darkness even Monte would not be able to tell what she was wearing. She moved without a sound along the dock in her bare feet until the shadowy hull of the *Hadley* loomed beside her. She called to Monte in a soft voice. There was no answer. She called again. Finally she boarded the boat and went forward through the deckhouse down to the sleeping quarters.

"Monte. Wake up." she called, feeling her way along the bunk until her hand touched his bare shoulder. She shook him hard.

"Ugh?" he grunted.

"Monte, wake up."

His head popped up. He stared at her in bewilderment. She was about to tell him that he was wanted on the telephone when his sleepy voice came to her less than a foot away.

"I thought I was dreaming, honey," he said. "What an angel you are to come back."

"There's a call—"

He smothered her words with a kiss as he pulled her up to him. She tried to push him away but his arms went around her. The phone call was driven from her mind while she struggled to get free. Carol groaned. She could not stop him. She could not move. This man was like no one she had ever met before. His throbbing desire struck an involuntary response in her. She stared wide-eyed in the darkness as her body began moving with desire. She forgot everything but the passion that overwhelmed her. Her resistance turned into eager yearning as she clung to him.

A few minutes later Carol felt his body shudder and a dam break in his loins. He held her tighter, more dependently, his breath coming hard in his throat, his head on her breast.

The stars were dying in the sky, and the first faint touch of dawn appeared as Carol retraced her steps along the dock much, much later. A cool, refreshing breeze blew across the river. Her emotions were an odd mix. She felt utter relaxation, pleasant weariness. She was embarrassed, of course, yet somehow her conscience was not tormenting her. *Is it because I love him?* she wondered. *Could I, after so short a time?*

Monte Abbot would never know; he would never believe the truth about her visit. She could not expect him to believe that she had come to him to tell him about a phone call. She shook her mussed brown curls in disbelief. What an odd turn this night had brought.

But she was smiling as she entered the club house and started toward her room. Then remembering, she veered toward the telephone booth. It gave her a vindictive satisfaction to hang up the receiver that had been left dangling. She chuckled as she wondered how long the arrogant woman at the other end had waited.

Carol was asleep the moment her head hit the pillow. She didn't even feel the cool, morning breeze whisper past an open window sill nearby, *Are you ready?*

3 Dinner on the Chase Park Plaza Roof

Carol overslept that warm and sunny morning and had to hurry through breakfast. This kind of weather always brought out boatmen. One of her best customers, Mr. K. G. Simpson, drove up just as she was finishing her coffee.

"Howdy, Miss Burke," he called to her. Simpson was a middle-aged man with a ruddy face. "I'm thinking of launching my boat into the river this weekend. Can I look at her?"

"Be right with you."

Carol gulped the rest of her coffee, got the keys to the boat and went out. She and Simpson shook hands and walked twenty yards to the shed, which was located at the edge of the river bank. Its wide doors opened onto a marine railway that sloped down to the water. This added expense for Carol saved time and money for the boat owner without making repairs in a dry dock. They went in.

"There she is, Mr. Simpson. I looked at her a few days ago. Everything seemed in order."

"Can we pull back the tarpaulin?" he asked.

Carol unfastened the covering and they rolled it back. Simpson's boat was a low, fast express cruiser, made of Honduras mahogany. He walked around it to examine the hull. He beamed with satisfaction, but then his expression grew thoughtful as he came back to Carol.

"I've decided to moor my boat at Grayson's Dock on the lake for the summer. That's why I'm anxious to get her launched as soon as possible."

"Oh." A pang of disappointment filled Carol, and then her blue-gray eyes filled with tears. She looked away. "I'm sorry you're leaving, Mr. Simpson. We'll miss you."

"I'll sure miss being here, too, believe me. I started with your dad years ago. He taught me how to handle the first boat I ever owned."

"We can get the boat operable by the weekend for you. I'll talk to Matt right away," said Carol. Simpson's lost patronage was a serious blow and cost her several hundred dollars for the summer.

"You know how things are, Miss Burke. I'm sorry to be going, but no one is boating here anymore. I wish your docks were north on Alton Lake."

"I know. I can't blame you."

"Why don't you move up there?"

"It would take a lot of money which I don't have. Besides, dad remained here so long that I'd sort of hate to move on."

Simpson made a quick smile. He had gotten an unpleasant chore off his mind. "Well, I'll be back Saturday morning. I'll need a lot of marine supplies to prepare for this spring before I leave, but we'll go into that in a few days."

She walked back to the clubhouse with him. He chatted with her before he got into his car and drove off. Bleakly she went back into the clubhouse and poured herself a second cup of coffee. In part, Monte Abbot's business would make up for the loss of Mr. Simpson, but not nearly enough. She did not know what she was going to do. At this rate, her creditors would be swarming all over the place within a month.

She was sitting on a stool at the counter, brooding over her financial woes, when Monte came in dressed in a summer-weight business suit and a bright bow tie.

"Good morning," he smiled at her intimately. "Could I buy some breakfast?"

"Will coffee and cinnamon rolls do?"

"I could eat a lot more than that after a grand night. But I wouldn't want to go anywhere else in the world."

She went behind the counter and poured him a cup of coffee. She pushed two rolls on a plate into a toaster oven, and then served him before returning to her stool beside him.

"Going into town?" she asked.

"Yes. I've got business to attend to. You said last night you have transportation."

"We've got a station wagon. Matt will drive you to the car line at Baden. You can take a street car or bus right into downtown St. Louis."

He gobbled down one of the rolls and finished the coffee. Then he smiled and lowered his voice.

"It was sweet of you to come to my boat last night, Carol."

A tinge of color crept into her cheeks. She wondered what he really thought of her. Any girl that did what she had done, so blatantly and openly, could not hope for any man's respect. Carol jumped up and poured more coffee for him.

"You may not believe it, but I didn't come back for that at all," she said, her face flushed.

"Of course not. But if you're half as glad as I am…"

"I came to tell you that you were wanted on the telephone."

Monte had raised his coffee cup and was about to take a sip. His eyebrows shot up at her words. He lowered the cup and looked around at her. The amusement faded from his eyes. "Who was it?"

"I don't know, she wouldn't give her name."

"Then it was a woman?"

"Yes."

"What did she say?"

"She asked me to call you to the phone. That's why I came down to the boat."

"But you didn't say anything about it."

"You didn't give me a chance," she told him reprovingly.

Monte smiled as they exchanged glances. "I'm glad I didn't." Then he was serious again.

"Did she say anything at all?"

"No, but I said plenty to her. I'm not in the habit of calling people to the phone at that hour of the night. All I can say is she had a good, long wait," said Carol.

"What? She held on while you came to get me?"

Carol nodded and Monte burst out laughing. The more he thought of it, the funnier it seemed. It took him several minutes to get back to normal.

"Do you know who it was?" she asked, hoping he would reveal the caller's identity.

"Yes, and I'll bet she's sizzling to this moment about being left holding the phone."

He said no more. The incident, somehow, improved Monte's spirits. He laughed and joked with Carol while finishing his breakfast. When he was ready to leave for St. Louis, she asked Matt to drive him in.

Carol welcomed a good mood and sense of relief after they left in the station wagon. The more she saw of Monte, the better she liked him. Her recollections of the previous night were pleasant indeed. He was a young man she could go for. There was no doubt that he belonged to the country club set – he dressed in imported cotton shirts, tailored khakis and genuine leather shoes. A barber styled his hair and manicured his nails.

Carol told herself in earnest not to get attracted to Monte for the money he appeared to have, although there was nothing repulsive about it. Her own dire financial predicament served only to emphasize that in her mind.

They were worlds apart socially. Yet, Carol had rubbed elbows with wealth before. She was at ease with river men and millionaires—especially millionaires who preferred the river to the golf course. Monte Abbot was in that category, she decided. Everything considered, his arrival at the Cabaret Boat Dock could not have been timelier. With that thought, Carol tackled her work with renewed vigor.

Activity increased on the dock. Two boat owners showed up to do some repair work on their crafts at noon. Carol completed work on her accounts and phoned in an order to the Marine Supply House for some paint, oakum caulking, grease and four new life jackets for the launch. This was the boat used to ferry folks to Cabaret Island. Fortunately, her credit was still good with Eddy Smith who ran the supply house. Carol kept so busy that the day was over before she knew it.

She was about to prepare dinner for herself when Monte drove up in a car. She stared at it in amazement. It was a shiny 1956 Cadillac convertible and looked brand new, with tail fins gleaming in the gathering dust.

"Did you buy that car today?" she asked, when he showed it to her.

"No. I leased this convertible for a few weeks. Have you had dinner yet?"

"I was just getting it started."

"Don't go any further. I want to take you to dinner."

"But—"

"Come on with me. Matt can look after this place for a few hours. How would a nice, thick steak suit you?"

Her mouth watered. She had not had a steak for weeks. She gave him a blinding smile as her resistance vanished. "I can't go dressed this way. I'll have to change," she said.

"Take your time. I've got to go onto the boat for a few minutes. Can you be ready in half an hour?"

She nodded, and the next instant he took off. A sudden thrill of excitement filled Carol. She had not been away from the dock for dinner for quite a while. She hurried to the boat shed, where Matt had been preparing Mr. Simpson's craft to launch in a few days, and told him she would be gone for the evening.

In her room she took a shower, gave careful attention to her face and hair then got into the best summer dress she owned. It was an apricot shantung frock with flowing skirt, bare back and halter neckline. She slipped into high-heeled black sling backs. This outfit pleased her with the effect as she stared at herself in the mirror.

Monte stared at her with open admiration when she came out to the car where he had been waiting. He looked her over from head to foot then gave a low whistle. "I knew you were a knockout, but I didn't know you could do it up this good."

She smiled radiantly as he held the car door open for her. A moment later they drove to Riverview Drive and headed into town. It was good to get away from the dock and the clubhouse for a change. Monte drove with assurance, and when he came to the traffic circle he swung around onto Kingshighway without hesitation.

"You know your way in St Louis?" she asked.

"Yes, I've been in the city before. Quite a number of times. But never came by boat on the Mississippi River before this trip."

"You have relatives here?" Carol was sure now, that she would learn something about him. She waited expectantly.

"Yes. Friends." That was all he said.

Then he went on, "I remember a swell place to eat on the top floor of a hotel near Forest Park. How would you like to go there?" he asked.

"I'd love it."

"You know where I mean?"

"Yes. The Zodiac—on the Chase Park Plaza Hotel roof."

"I can see you've been around." He smiled and patted her knee.

Carol was more pleased than ever with Monte Abbott. She had been into town several times with Joe in the past month or so. His favorite eating places were always down along the river front on the landing: Schwartz's, Skippers' Inn, and Skeeters. She inevitably drank beer with Joe and ate huge servings of sauerkraut and sausage. It would be a pleasure to get away from that.

At eight o'clock that evening, Carol and Monte sat at a table for two in the Zodiac Room on the Chase Roof, sipping champagne cocktails while their steaks were being prepared to order. A string orchestra provided subdued background music. On the street, far below, the night traffic ebbed and flowed. The lights on the drives in Forest Park made glittering, curved necklaces on a canopy of velvet.

"You've told me so little about yourself," said Carol, hoping to invite Monte to talk about himself.

"There's very little to tell. Besides, you're far more interesting."

"But you know a lot more about me. You've seen where I live and work."

"You know something about me. I like the river and boats –and I like you. What more do you want to know?"

I guess that's a good deal, at that, Carol thought.

"I might have become an architect, but I went into the Navy instead. After my discharge, I couldn't stand the idea of going back to the university. Anyway, complications arose. I'm not doing anything at the moment, but that's not too important. I'm with an awfully pretty girl right now who's a lot more fun to talk about."

"Okay," she laughed. "I won't get curious about you again."

Their steaks were served and Carol ate until she was thoroughly satiated. Monte insisted on brandy with their coffee afterward, and then in a short while they were dancing. Their bodies pressed together as they moved in rhythm to the music. Carol felt wonderful. She wanted the evening to go on forever with

"I Could Have Danced all Night" from that new musical *My Fair Lady* ringing in her ears.

"Do you know what I want to do with you tomorrow?" he asked when they were back at the table. Monte's hands covered hers. "Let's get aboard the *Hadley* and take a day excursion for ourselves up on the Alton Lake."

"I can't. There's too much to do around the dock."

"Please, Carol," he begged. "Later on I might not get the chance. There're a few things cooking that might take considerable time while I'm here".

Carol did not like the sound of that. She wanted to get to know him better. She wanted him to know her. How could a girl look after a dock when there was a man around who might hold the key to her future happiness?

"I don't see how I can get away for a whole day, Monte," she said with concern.

"Just walk off. That's the way to do it. Things can't be that urgent."

"If only you knew," she said, thinking of the charges she had run up at the marine supply house.

"Please come with me, Carol. You said it doesn't take long to cruise up there. We could leave early and be back by evening."

She stared at the twinkling lights on the streets and in Forest Park below them in the night. She wanted to go with him. She would enjoy a day away from the dock and the headaches that went with it. Frank Weaver, Joe Mosley, and all the rest---everyone had demands on her except Monte Abbott. His demands were the kind she liked. *What if I did run off for a day? The dock would still be here when I get back.*

Suddenly her gut took over. "Hell, why not?" she said.

4   Stranded on Alton Lake

Carol and Monte backed the *Hadley* out of the slip at eight o'clock the next morning with Monte at the wheel. But she stood beside him, in shorts and yachting cap coaching him on the trick of getting away from the dock. They had a clear day for their trip to the Alton Lake. She still felt a little guilty about running off and leaving the responsibility of the dock to Matt, but one day would not hurt, she kept telling herself.

Once the cruiser was out in the current, Monte opened her up, and the Cabaret Dock quickly fell behind. They hugged the Missouri shore for a mile or so, and then crossed over with the channel to the Illinois side, just below the Chain-of-Rocks Bridge. As they passed the intake tower of the St Louis Waterworks, Carol leaned out of the cabin and waved to a man bent over a guard rail. He waved back, not recognizing her at such a distance across the water.

"Someone you know?" Monte asked.

"Yes, it's Vernon Flynn. He's worked there for years."

With the bridge behind them, they made a straight run up the channel to the confluence of the Missouri and Mississippi Rivers. Carol pointed out the starting point of the Lewis and Clark

Expedition in 1804 and The Bellefontaine Cemetery to the west where William Clark and many other famous persons were laid to rest. She showed him the oil refineries of Roxana and Wood River; and then the Alton Slough, where steam boats were tied up in the marsh during the winter in the old days. By mid-morning, they were at the lock of the huge roller dam, Number Twenty-Six.

"Here's where we'll have some fun," she said.

"Pretty tricky getting through, eh?"

"No, but they hate to put a small boat through by itself. Where's your horn?"

Monte showed her. She blasted a signal on it, and then went aft to the cockpit for a look up to the top of the massive, concrete lock. A surprised engineer was staring down at her.

"We want through." she yelled up at him.

"You'll have to wait There's a towboat coming along in about an hour. We'll put you through at the same time."

"That's what you think, buster. We're coming in the lock, and I'll report you if you don't give us passage right now. While you're at it, lower us a rope. We don't want to smash our hull while you guys are stalling." With that she went back into the cabin.

"Do you think they'll do what you said?" Monte asked with uncertainty. He was amused at the way she asserted herself, like a peppery old river hand. The fact that she was so young and enticing made the contrast all the more interesting.

"They'd better. We'll have some more fun when we get to the top. You'd better go back and catch the rope. I'll stay at the wheel."

Carol eased the boat into the lock. A rope was lowered to them. Monte stood in the cockpit, holding onto it, so that the *Hadley* would not drift. The enormous steel gates closed behind them. The water inside the locks began to bubble and churn as water from above the dam flooded in.

Twenty minutes later the *Hadley* rose to the level of the lake behind the dam. Carol glanced toward the upper rim of the lock.

Herb Yost, the lock master, a gruff character in his early sixties, was standing there waiting to reprimand the rude owner of this cruiser. He looked sternly at Monte, who stood in the cockpit.

"Maybe you don't know the rules young fellow," he called. "We can't be putting through every rowboat that comes along. Now, by golly, you remember that or—."

"Aw, go on." Carol stuck her head out of the window by the wheel and grinned at Herb. "We'll come through whenever we please, and you'd damn well better give us good service."

Herb's head jerked around in astonishment. When he saw who it was, he put his fists on his hips. A broad smiled crossed his face.

"I might have known somebody was playing a trick. What are you doing up here, Carol?"

"I came up for a look around the lake. I want to see how the other half lives," she said.

"Going to move your gear up here this summer? We could sure use somebody like you on this lake," he called back to her fondly.

"Not me. I'm staying where the river moves like it ought to."

"Don't ever think I wouldn't like to be there myself, girl," said Herb. "But times have changed, you know. When are you coming back through?"

"This afternoon," said Carol.

He turned to an assistant who was standing nearby. "For her we can overlook a rule once in a while. Let that little gal through any time she wants. I used to be a cub in the pilot house with her father, old Sam Burke. He knew more about this river than you'll ever know if you live to be a hundred." He looked over at Carol. "Good seeing you again. I'll drop in the next time I get down below the Chain-of-Rocks."

The upriver gates swung open. Monte let his end of the rope go and joined Carol in the cabin. He opened the throttle, and the *Hadley* picked up speed on the Alton Lake.

"I thought for a while those fellows back at the lock were going to start throwing things at me," he said.

Carol laughed. "I've known Herb Yost for years."

"Maybe you have, but I'm new in his life. If I ever come this way alone, they'll probably make me haul the *Hadley* around the dam on my back."

They cruised up the lake, having lunch out of the galley on the way. By the middle of the afternoon they were many miles above the dam and north of Grafton where the Illinois River enters the Mississippi. It had grown quite warm, and the water looked inviting.

"Do you suppose we could drop anchor somewhere long enough for a swim?" Monte asked.

"I was just thinking of that myself," she replied. Her eyes squinted across the water, in search of an appropriate spot for a swim. She pointed to a place quite a distance out of the channel. Monte headed the boat to the spot she indicated.

Carol was not too sure of the depths and suggested he cut the motor to take the *Hadley* in slowly. Half an hour later they lowered anchor. It came to rest in about ten feet of water. They stood offshore about fifty yards, and from the looks of things this remote spot on the lake was as removed from civilization as the moon.

Carol tossed a piece of paper on the water and watched its direction.

"If it falls astern, we'd better take turns having a swim," she said.

"But why? We'd feel pretty silly if there was a current, and we couldn't make it back to the boat."

The paper floated close to the boat, and Carol announced that they would be safe to go in together. Monte dropped a tiny rope ladder over the stern, to use in case of difficulty getting back aboard. Then he went in the cabin and changed into his bathing trunks. Carol changed into her black, Bikini-style suit.

When Monte caught a glimpse of her, poised on the stern, the sun glinting on her superb body he gasped in appreciation of her beauty.

She turned, flashed him a smile and executed a neat dive, disappearing into the water with barely a splash. He ran to the stern and looked down. Her chestnut-brown head broke the surface a few yards away. She turned and waved gaily to him. "Come on in. The water's wonderful," she called.

Monte joined her. Carol was an expert swimmer. She cut the water with a sure and graceful overhand stroke, her small feet kicking up a bubbling wake, like a paddle wheel. It was all he could do to keep up with her.

"Say, I didn't know you were that good," he cried.

"I'd have drowned before I was five if I hadn't learned to swim. That's one thing you've got to know if you live on the river," she said.

"You act like you lived in it, not on it."

She laughed and splashed water at him. He reached for her, but she disappeared beneath the surface. He paddled around in a circle, waiting for her to come up. Finally, when her head appeared, back near the *Hadley,* he swam toward her.

Carol dived again. She felt for the hull of the boat and swam under it, coming up on the other side. She laughed to herself as she heard Monte splashing around. He called to her. She peeked around the bow of the boat, just long enough to be seen. When he started for her again, she swam under water to the stern, scrambled up the rope, and ducked into the cabin.

She was dressed in her shorts and halter when Monte climbed over the stern in to the cockpit.

He smiled as he came to her. "You really gave me a chase, but try and get out of this."

He took her in his arms and gave her a crushing kiss. Carol moaned at the touch of his lips. She let him draw her against his damp body. They clung to each other as if magnetized. In the exhilaration of the moment, she sensed a throbbing in him, one that added to her growing hope that she might come to mean more to Monte than a mere passing fancy.

"We've got to get on our way back," she said, pushing him away several minutes later.

"But it's still early. Let's have a drink."

"Okay, but we ought to start back before long, Monte."

"We will, baby," he said, patting her shoulder.

They took their drinks up on the deckhouse and sat in the sun. The first highball was so pleasant, and the sun so warm and comfortable that they had another. A delightful drowsiness followed. Carol fought it for a while, and then gave in. Monte's hand stroked her arm, and she dropped off to sleep.

When she opened her eyes, she knew instantly that it was late. The sun was low in the sky. She blinked toward the west. A water crane skimmed the river in the distance, its great wings flapping, as it looked for an evening meal. She turned to Monte, who was lying face down, at her side.

"Hey, wake up. We've got to get going. Quick."

Monte rose up. It took him a moment to gain full consciousness. "What time is it?"

"Too late to fool around another minute. Come on. Night fall is just around the corner."

She was angry at herself for letting this happen. He grumbled good-naturedly as they went down to the cabin. Monte started the motor, and she crawled out on the bow to raise the anchor.

"Come forward with it," she called back to him.

Mindful of the urgency for getting back to the dock, he put the boat into forward top speed. It was over the anchor before Carol realized what had happened. She did not have time to warn him. She heaved at the anchor with all her might. It gave, but did not come entirely free. Thinking the anchor was out of the water, Monte swung the wheel hard toward starboard. Carol nearly lost her balance as the port side of the boat pushed against the anchor rope. She yelled frantically to him to slow down as she pulled.

"Cut the motor." she yelled at the top of her lungs as the rope jerked in her hands.

Monte suddenly realized what he had done. In his haste to head the *Hadley* around toward the channel, he had swung into the anchor rope. The motor caught, then raced, then caught again. A groaning noise came from the stern. He cut the motor.

Carol hurled the rope over the deck house and ran back to the cockpit. She and Monte got there at the same time. He tugged at the rope as she looked on with a sick feeling.

"It's fouled in the propeller," he said. She nodded feebly.

"Sorry, Carol. I knew better than to do that," he said contritely.

"Well, let's get at it. Maybe there's not too much damage done. I'll go down and—"

"You'll do nothing of the sort. I'll go." He stared at her. There was not one girl in a million who would know what to do in a case like this, much less be willing to tackle it. Carol was that one girl.

"Just get in the water and untangle that rope. I can't stay here all night," she grumbled.

Monte was over the side in a flash. Carol leaned over the stern, trying to see down through the water as he lowered himself to the propeller. He worked for a minute, then came up for air.

"Is it pretty bad?" she asked.

"It's wrapped around the shaft, tight as a drum." Before she could say more he went down again. She could feel him tugging desperately at the rope. When he came up, he was panting.

"Have you got a knife? Maybe we could cut it.," she said.

"There's one in the galley."

She went to the galley and came back with a large, sharp knife. Monte had gotten his breath. She handed him the knife. He filled his lungs with air and disappeared below the surface again. When he came up he spat out a mouthful of water.

When his breathing slowed down, he looked up at her sadly. "I got part of it cut away, but the rest won't budge."

"Come back aboard, and let me have a go at it."

Reluctantly he climbed up on the stern. Carol did not even bother getting out of her shorts. She took the knife from him and slipped into the water. She filled her lungs with air and down she went. Her hands felt their way back to the shaft. Her fingers closed over the rope that was entangled about the casing. She sawed on it with the knife. She repeated this, coming up for air three times.

They still had not managed to get rid of all the rope. They turned the engine over, but it did no good. Both tried again. One strand remained firmly coiled about the shaft, jamming the rod so that it would not budge. At last they stood together on the *Hadley* as darkness came to the river.

"Looks like we're stuck her for the night," Monte observed.

Forgetting herself, Carol screamed, "God damn it. How'd this happen?" When he looked at her with amused astonishment, she broke off, ashamed of herself.

She was not angered at having to spend the night on the lake with Monte. The trouble was such an escapade could not possibly go unnoticed. She knew there would be talk among the river men. Few would believe that she had not remained with him deliberately.

5   Joe and Monte SPAR

The *Hadley* was found the following morning at seven o'clock by a tug, piloted by Jim Norton. Jim was a slender man with a roving eye and trim mustache. Carol had known him a long time. "What're you up to?" he called.

Norton towed them to Frank Perrine's boat works at Alton. They lifted the *Hadley* from the water with a stiff leg derrick and freed the propeller shaft of the last remnants of the anchor rope.

Herb Yost greeted them, on their return trip through the lock, with thoughtful quietness. He knew they had been on the lake all night. Carol and Monte got back to the Cabaret Dock at noon.

Carol attempted to ease her nagging conscience with hard work during the next four days. Fortunately, she was not distracted by Monte. He was in town most of the time, on business. Carol admitted to herself that she had no regrets spending the night on the lake with him. The river men who found out about it would think the worst. In a way, they would be right. She regretted that, but the night on the lake had not been her fault.

She was in her room behind the clubhouse, after a strenuous day, when a knock came at her door. She had eaten dinner late and sat in a chair, reading, her feet propped on the table. The radio was turned low to a Rock 'n Roll Dance Party on the CBS Radio Network. She usually listened to Rosemary Clooney, Doris Day or her favorite "Lonely Girl" by Julie London. Today's program was featuring this new guy, Elvis Presley and his "Heartbreak Hotel."

"Come in," she called, looking up from her book.

"Hi Carol." It was Joe. He sauntered in, tossing his cap to the table and made himself comfortable in a chair.

"Is your job down by the Meramec finished already?" she asked.

"Nope. I got the night off. Thought we might have a beer somewhere."

"Not me. I'm too tired."

He smiled with a smirk. "Too tried from what?"

"We put Mr. Simpson's express cruiser in the river today. On top of that, Matt and I painted the launch. I've been going hard since I got up this morning."

"That shouldn't have tired you out," he remarked with a peculiar inflection in his voice. "But if we can't go away from here, what's to stop us from having a drink anyway?"

"I haven't got any liquor, that's why," she retorted.

"I've got a bottle in my car."

Without waiting to see if she approved, Joe got up. He came back with a bottle of whiskey. At the counter in the clubhouse he mixed two drinks and brought them into her room.

"I didn't say I wanted a drink," Carol said.

"You don't have to drink it."

Something was on Joe's mind. She did not like the way he was acting. She did not like the way his glance was moving over her body.

"If you've got any ideas about tonight, Joe, get them out of your head right now. I told you, I was worn out," she warned.

"Yeah, I know. You probably are. But how much of it is from working around the dock?"

"Just what do you mean by that?" She sat forward and looked at him closely.

"I've been hearing things about you. Things I don't like." Joe sipped his drink.

"What things?"

"You went up to the lake with a fellow in a boat cruiser and spent the night. Seems as though everybody on the river knows about it by now."

"All right, so I did. We went up one morning and intended getting back that afternoon. We jammed a propeller, and it was early the next morning before anyone found us. Jim Norton picked us up when he came by in his tug. Is there anything wrong with that?"

"No, I guess a jammed propeller is about as good an excuse as any."

"I don't like that crack," she shot back. "It's none of your damn business what I do. But it so happens that is the truth. Next time you get to Alton, stop in at Perrine's boat works. He lifted the *Hadley* out of the water and helped us untangle a rope from the propeller shaft. He saw what had happened."

"Maybe you got into trouble. I wouldn't know. But as for it being none of my business, that's where you're wrong." Joe's face darkened.

"Since when do you have a right to tell me what to do?" she demanded, her eyes blazing.

"I've got the right to smash a guy's face in when he starts messing around with my girl." His words were quiet, but ominous.

Carol studied him carefully. She chose her reply with caution because she did not want any trouble with Joe. "You'll not start any fight around here. I'm running a business. I'd have a patrol car from Riverview Drive over here the minute you tried. Don't forget that."

"I'm not going to let you kick up any more scandal. Two nights ago at the Skipper's Inn, I had to blacken a fellow's eye because he made a wisecrack about you. You're getting tagged as a hot number. That's what happened as a result of your visit to the lake."

"I can't help what people say. That wasn't my fault," Carol said sullenly.

"No, but you can help it from now on. You stay away from that fellow, Abbott, do you hear?"

"I'll see who I please. Besides, Monte Abbott is a customer here. A good one, I might add."

"He won't be when I get through with him," Joe said thinly. Their eyes locked. A cold smile crossed Joe's lips. He came over and grabbed hold of her.

"Let go of me." Carol cried.

"You know how it's been between us, Carol. All of a sudden you're trying to go high hat. Well, I'm not holding still for it."

His powerful arms tightened around her. It was not the first time Carol found she could not match his strength. She could not even come close. He kissed her, bruising her lips. There had been times when she had not minded his French-style kisses, but now the feel of his mouth and tongue on hers filled her with revulsion. He bent her toward him. She endured it as long as she could. Then she struggled fiercely and managed to turn her face away. Her eyes filled with contempt. "If you're through, let me go." she snapped

"I didn't say I was done," he grinned.

"Oh no, you don't. Not that." as he put his mouth on the side of her neck. She said, her voice rising, "Let loose."

She struggled in his arms. He made it a game of cat-and-mouse. Carol could not possibly get free. Her fury mounted as his caresses became more eager. Panic and desperation came over her as he held her so tight she could not move. She gouged at his face with her finger nails. Joe yelled, "Jesus Christ." and released her. He was breathing hard, and his eyes were stormy.

"It's that Monte Abbott. He's the one who's changed you," Joe accused.

"Get out of here. I'm fed up. All you ever wanted from me was a place to hang your hat."

"You think you're going to hook a rich guy who can afford a fancy yacht, just for fun. That's what you're after, ain't it?" he said sarcastically.

"If it is, that's my business."

"You're not going to marry him. You're going to marry me."

"I wouldn't marry you or any other river man. Even if you 'all were the only kind left on earth. Get out."

Carol stood up, straightened her hair and shot him an angry glance.

Joe glared back at her. Things had gone his own way for a long time around the Cabaret Boat Dock. He didn't intend to let a stranger muscle in on him. Carol Burke belonged to him. He started toward her again.

There was a knock at the door as Monte Abbott walked in. He was unaware of the tense situation. He smiled pleasantly at Joe. "Hello there. Haven't seen you around for a while, Mosley."

"No, but you've been around plenty, from what I hear," Joe retorted. His hostile eyes burned.

Monte glanced at him with surprise. Then he gave a shrug and looked at Carol. She lost no time getting between the two men. Joe was in a fighting mood, she knew.

"I had hoped to get back early tonight, Carol," said Monte. "I was thinking we might have dinner together, but I suppose you've eaten by now."

"Yes. Some time ago."

"So that's why you wouldn't have a beer with me?" Joe spoke up. He looked around to Carol coldly. "You were waiting for him."

"You don't know what you're talking about. I wasn't waiting for him. I wasn't waiting for anybody."

"She's right. Carol and I had made no plans, if that's what bothers you," Monte interjected.

"Stay out of this." Joe growled.

"Well, now look, old boy. Let's be reasonable. You can't take it out on Carol, when it's not her fault." Monte's tone tried to pacify.

Joe glared at him contemptuously. "I figured you to be a panty weight the first time I saw you. Now I know."

Half-smiling, Joe reached over and gave Monte a vicious shove. It came unexpectedly, and Monte was caught off balance. He tripped over a chair and sprawled on the floor. Joe laughed.

"There'll be no more of that." Carol cried, grabbing Joe's arm and pulling him back.

Joe had no intention of following up. He thought Monte Abbott was afraid. He smiled disdainfully.

"What do you mean---pulling a trick like that?" Carol raged.

"Maybe that'll show you what sort of weak-livered catfish you've been prancing around with."

Monte got back to his feet and regained his composure. An apologetic smile was on his lips. Carol didn't know what to think. She did not want a fight here, but it sickened her to see the whimpering look on Monte's face. She did not like brutes, like Joe, but neither did she like weaklings. Then a tornado struck the room.

Monte's fist shot out. It exploded on Joe Mosley's jaw. Joe's eyes went wide with astonishment. With a howl he raised his arms. He rushed at Monte like an enraged bull. Carol tried to scream, but nothing came from her throat. It was sealed tight with fear. She recoiled against a wall.

Joe's charge ended abruptly. Monte caught him on the chin again with a twisted smashing right. Before Joe knew what was happening, Monte's left landed on his nose. Joe stopped in his tracks. He had run into a buzz-saw. He struck out blindly, but his blows went wild as Monte bore in. Joe staggered back, and Monte followed, hammering at his jaw with fists that moved with the force and speed of a machine gun.

Joe's eyes glazed. His shoulders sagged, and his arms hung limp at his sides. Monte landed one more blow. Joe's knees buckled and he folded up on the floor like a sack of potatoes.

"Sorry I had to do that, Carol," Monte remarked casually.

She stared at him, her mouth open. She gazed down at Joe on the floor, in disbelief. Nothing like this had ever happened to Joe Mosley. She sprang into action and ran to the lunch counter and came back with a cold towel. Monte lifted Joe to a chair and Carol put the towel on his face.

In a few minutes Joe regained his senses. He shook the cobwebs from his mind. His eyes filled with hate as he looked up. He was ready for another try.

"That's all," Carol announced, standing between them. "If either of you tries to fight again, I'm calling the police." Her tone left no doubt.

"We won't," Monte assured her.

"I'll get even with you, Abbott, if it takes me the rest of my life." Joe announced tight-lipped. He stood up.

Monte smiled. "No hard feelings as far as I'm concerned."

"Well, that doesn't go for me, see?"

"I'm warning you both," said Carol, glancing from one to the other. "Don't you dare start fighting again."

"Want to step outside, Abbott? I dare you," Joe challenged.

"Oh. I won't have it. Not here." Carol shoved a bar stool into the counter.

Monte glanced at his opponent. "Let's not upset her any more tonight, old boy. You and I can get together another time."

"Think you're pretty smart, don't you? Okay, well see about that," Joe sneered.

A smile of contempt crossed Joe's face. He picked up his cap. He tossed Carol a serious glance, then left.

She did not relax until she heard Joe's car roar away from the clubhouse. Then she turned and looked at Monte, curiosity and wonder in her blue eyes. Until now she had not realized the strength and courage behind his easygoing exterior.

"The only reason I didn't accommodate Joe was because of you," he said.

"I know. Thanks a lot, Monte." A smile crept across her lips. She felt energized, not as tired as she had been earlier in the evening.

"I'm wondering if you'd care to go with me on a drive along Riverview Drive, then for a bite to eat afterward. We can go aboard the *Hadley* if you'd like." There was twinkle in his eye

"I think that would be fun."

There was a twinkle in Carol's eyes too when she answered, and a flutter in her heart. It was not Monte's money or boat that made her feel that way. She could say that now.

6 Frank comes to Collect

As the river's crest was falling, Cabaret Island's sandbars lay warm and inviting in the summer sun. Carol had already ferried several parties of picnickers to the island for a day on the fine beaches. She prepared to cross again with a party of eight as Matt helped her customers on the dock board the launch.

The island had become a refuge for Canadian geese, teal and mallards: a safe harbor along their never ending river migration corridor. The colorful flamingoes stood on one leg as they patiently fished the shallow edges of the water. With the channel low, red fox and white-tailed deer had been spotted swimming across to the sanctuary. Its thick growth of native cedar and birch trees twittered and rustled, the only clue to the hidden world of nature.

Conservationists had received permission to place bluebirds, the state-bird of Missouri, into low trees with small wooden habitats they liked to call home. These shy azure winged jewels were thriving. Their glorious song joined the chorus.

When Carol came out of the clubhouse, Frank Weaver stood at the edge of the steps, looking down at the activity. He looked around at her as she approached.

"Looks like business has picked up," he said.

"A little," she admitted.

"Just thought I'd run out and see how things were going. I'd like to have a talk with you, Carol."

"Sorry. There's a party waiting for me to take them across the river to the island."

Ordinarily, the sight of Frank Weaver would have plunged her into a sober mood, but not today. Carol felt wonderful. After last night she could face Weaver with confidence. She could face anything. Her newly-discovered love for Monte gave her courage. No one could hurt her now.

"Believe I'll ride along with you," said Frank.

Carol shrugged and went down the steps. Frank followed her - hounding her at the wheel of the launch. The noisy passengers sat up forward, raucous and eager for an afternoon on the beach. Matt cast off the lines, and Carol backed the launch away from the dock. A moment later, she headed across the river.

"Business ought to be good with all the free advertising you're getting," said Frank.

"What do you mean?"

"I'm not so dumb about what goes on around here. Just be thankful I haven't snitched to the trustees."

"What are you talking about?" she demanded.

"You," said Frank.

At that moment she had to shift her attention to a tow of oil barges coming down river. By the time she had cleared the barges, the launch was approaching the landing at Cabaret Island. She brought the boat in slowly and discharged the passengers. Then she and Frank started back across the river.

"Okay now," she said. "Suppose you come to the point."

"The point is you seem to be looking for more than one business. I've heard some comments about you. They ain't pretty. For instance, I heard you had fun up on the Alton Lake, even spent the night, when you should've been tending business at the Dock."

"Mind your own damn business. I'll take care of mine."

"It just so happens looking after the interests of the Ebbs Estate for the trustees is my business. They're not going to let you manage the Cabaret Dock when you find it more fun to spend the night out with one of your customers."

"Don't you talk to me like that." she snapped.

Frank ignored her warning. "Don't think I haven't learned what sort of girl you are. I happen to know some river people. They all say the same thing. You're not trying to make a go of the business. You're more interested in men."

"How dare you!" she warned. "But, yes I date."

"And I'm here to say you're not going to keep it up much longer unless—"

"Unless what?" she demanded.

Frank paused. His eyes roved over her. Her bare legs and the enticing outlines of her sweater made his blood race. He licked his upper lip then smirked. "You know what," he said.

"Why - of all the damn nerve." She slapped him so sharply that he jumped back. Frank scowled and came at her again. He jerked her away from the wheel. Carol fought out of his grasp, her face livid with fury. "Don't you dare touch me again." she warned.

"You're playing around with others when I'm the one you should pay attention to. I could ruin you," Frank gritted his teeth.

Carol grabbed a wrench that lay on the seat by the wheel. "You touch me one more time, and I'll land this on your head."

"Now look Carol," he said, modifying his tone into reconciliation. "There's no use getting that way."

"Oh, no? If you've got nerve enough to make a proposition to me, don't think I haven't got the nerve to bash your head in."

"That's no way for you to talk, considering how lenient I've been with you."

"Listen to me," said Carol shaking the wrench at him. "You've been threatening me with foreclosure long enough. I'm sick and tired of it. Go ahead and do your damnedest. See if I care. This place will close if I leave here. If that's what the trustees want, I'll call the bank and ask if this will be alright with them. They had wanted to protect the island as a natural preserve for wildlife. As for you, don't think for one minute that you can force me into anything."

"That does it." Frank cried. "I'll have you kicked off of the property within a week." His eyes blazed with frustration. "Your only chance will be to make a substantial payment against the loan."

"Or make a payment to you in a different way," she added arching her back in defiance.

He glanced at her. Frank's desire for this girl had been building up over a period of months. He had been unable to get her off his mind. At night she haunted his dreams, making sleep impossible. In trying to force her, he had thrown caution to the wind. If the trustees found out what he had been attempting to do, it would mean his job, but he no longer cared; if only he could have her. He clutched at her word now, hopeful that she was weakening.

"That's it," he nodded. "You'll pay one way or the other, or else." His tone softened. "You know how I feel about you, honey. I'm not so hard to take if you'll just give me a chance. That's why I'm insisting this is no life for you, Carol. Let me take care of you. You won't have to worry about mortgages or money or the damn river."

Carol fought down an impulse to slap him again. She hated his kind. Frank Weaver was mean, narrow minded and contemptible, but a sudden sense of caution warned her against arousing his hostility any further. She did not think he was bluffing this time. She believed what he said, that he would take Cabaret Boat Dock and Island away from her within the week. Her insides fell to liquid, seemed to foam up and force away her breath. She was four-years-old again, small and scared.

She needed time to overcome her fears, just as she did after her mother died when she was four-years-old.

Though Monte had confessed his love for her last night, he had not proposed marriage. Carol was keenly aware of that, yet thought a proposal was not far off. Once she was certain of Monte, Frank Weaver and all the rest could do anything they wanted. They would not be able to hurt her. She would be safe. The Mississippi

River could start running backwards after that, for all she cared, as it did after an earthquake in 1890.

Carol brought the launch to the dock. She said nothing to Frank. He left the boat with her and stood beside her on the dock by the gasoline pump. His eyes were speculative.

"Have you decided to think it over, Carol?" he asked with hesitation.

She looked across the river, her eyes distant and unseeing. "You said you'd have me out of here in a week. Well, I guess you can."

"I'd rather have it the other way. You could stay on, you know. Why do you want to think it over?"

"Maybe I will, for a week."

Frank's small eyes lit up. Carol had weakened, all right. No doubt about it. He smiled at her slyly. "Now you're beginning to show some sense. I'll be around again in a few days." With that Frank walked along the dock and up the steps.

The fool. Nothing on earth could force her to bestow her favors on Frank Weaver. He was crazy to think he could buy her. In a showdown she would give up the Cabaret Dock before she would ever let him lay a hand on her. Frank Weaver was no man. He was like milk toast.

One thing that he had said disturbed her, however. She did not like the inference that people were gossiping about her. Her father's name had been respected on the river, and Carol was proud of that. She did not want to be talked about. She had done nothing to deserve it. Her stranded overnight trip to the Alton Lake with Monte had been unfortunate. It had exposed her to a criticism which was not entirely justified. She had not gone there to spend the night with him. People would see how wrong they were when she and Monte announced their engagement. That thought carried her through the rest of the day.

Monte was in St. Louis on business, and he was spending the night in the Central West End with friends. Carol had plenty to do, as she looked forward to the evening, when she could get to bed early for a good long sleep.

At seven o'clock that night Carol hauled the last boatload of picnickers back from Cabaret Island. They were a tired but happy group, relaxed from a day away from the factory and their homes. If Carol got nothing else out of operating the clubhouse and boat dock, she found an abiding satisfaction in contributing to the enjoyment of others.

Joe Mosley was standing on the dock when the launch pulled in. She looked at him suspiciously as the expanse of water between the launch and the dock narrowed. *What could he want?* After her passengers were out of the boat, she gave the forward compartment a swift once-over to see that nothing had been left behind. Then she stepped to the dock as Matt came aboard to clean up.

"What are you doing this evening?" Joe asked.

"What's it to you?"

He gave a mirthless smile. "Could be I'd take you to a dinner somewhere. Don't you get tired of Wally's cooking?"

Wally Salinsbury was the short-order fry cook who managed the lunch counter for her in the daytime. Carol was not prepared to argue the point. It went without saying that she did. Wally had little imagination. All of his food tasted the same after the first week.

"I'm surprised you have the nerve to show up back here," she said.

"Maybe I wouldn't, except that I've got news for you."

"What about?"

"Let's go some place for dinner. I'll tell you then."

"I'm not interested."

"You'll be interested plenty in what I've got to say." he assured her. "Go on. Wash up and change. I'll take you to the Red Coach Inn on the highway."

"If you've got something to tell me, say it here."

"Nope, you'll have to wait."

"Is it about me?"

"It certainly concerns you."

Something in his tone caused her to think again before turning him down. She studied him carefully. He had news, alright. She could tell by his attitude. He smiled smugly as he looked back at her.

"Okay, I'll go with you," she said abruptly. Since Monte would not be here tonight, she saw no harm in having dinner with Joe to find out why he was looking so pleased with himself.

She went to the clubhouse and changed her clothes. She came out half an hour later in a simple, polished-cotton summer dress and high-heeled shoes. Every so often it did her good to get out of her shorts. She had not dressed for Joe tonight. She had dressed for herself. It made her feel like a woman, a human being again.

Joe drove on the toll bridge that went from St. Louis to Hartford, Illinois, over the Chain of Rocks Bridge, and then north on Highway 3 to the Red Coach Inn, a tavern near Alton. They sat in a leather-backed booth and ordered fried chicken. Joe ordered highballs for them while they waited for their food.

"What's all the news you said you had?" Carol asked, looking at him closely across the table.

Joe looked smug. "How much do you know about this fellow, Monte Abbott?"

At the mention of Monte's name, Carol stiffened. Joe had something on his mind. She knew it for sure now. She thought for a moment. She still knew very little about Monte, but she was not going to give Joe the satisfaction of finding that out.

"I know enough," she said haughtily.

"You do? And you're still willing to play around with him?" Joe smirked.

"Just what are you driving at?" Carol demanded.

"I've found out some things about that bird. He's making a sucker out of you."

"Monte's a gentleman," she replied with a high-minded attitude. "Furthermore, he's got the decency not to run me down, like a lot of men I know who are only out for what they can get."

"That so?" Joe smiled. He held her in suspense for a few moments. Then casually he said, "Maybe if you know so much about him, what I have to say won't be news."

"Probably not. And if you brought me here just to act smart and look as if you know everything, you're not going to get anywhere with it. Either come to the point, or shut up about Monte."

"Okay. I thought you might be interested in what I found out today, but you probably already know. So you shouldn't be surprised when I tell you that Monte Abbott has a wife."

She was not only surprised as Joe lowered the boom on her; she was stunned. Her breath caught, couldn't make it all the way down her lungs. It was as if a malignant mass pressed again her heart and chest, threatened to choke her. And it kept on growing, twisting her gut, an unbearable pressure.

"Her name is Hadley."

7 Monte's a Two-Timer

Carol never knew how she got through the meal at the Red Coach Inn with Joe. Her body seemed to function while her mind whirled in chaos. They were there for an hour, and while Carol went through the motions of eating, the food had no taste—it might as well have been cardboard.

Joe waited after exploding his bombshell, and then casually started talking of other things. She replied only in monosyllables. She could not keep her mind on what he was saying. She could think of nothing but the overpowering realization that Monte was married.

It all added up. She could see that now. No wonder he had told her nothing about himself. He could not have done that and still made use of her in the way he wanted. Carol felt as if all the supports in her life had been jerked out from under her. When she and Joe had finished dinner and got up from the booth, she did not think that her legs would support her.

She felt no gratitude toward Joe for his revelation. He had planned this well since he sprung the news on her with fiendish delight, only to leave her in her own torment. The only decent thing was that he made no attempt to impose himself on her agony. He drove back to the clubhouse through the night, and when he got there gave no indication that he wanted to come in. Joe had an insulting, self-satisfied smile on his face when she thanked him for the dinner.

"It was a pleasure," he said. "It certainly was."

Their glances met. She knew why it was a pleasure for him to hurt her about as much as he could. She looked away, heartsick. All she wanted now was to be alone so she could sort out her thoughts and see if she could make any sense of her troubles.

"See you later," she said and turned to the club house.

"You sure will. I'll be back-and next time you'll be glad to see me." With that he got back into his car and drove away.

Carol walked through the clubhouse in a daze. She closed the door of her room and locked it. She shuffled across to the bed and sank down on the edge. Monte—married? That thought overwhelmed her so much, that her brain felt as if it was in a vise, holding her to that one realization.

As she grappled with the information, her body broke into a cold sweat. Her emotions charged back and forth between anger and despair. *If I could just talk to him now* she thought. How could Monte be so cruel to her, yet he had been. He had seemed a gentleman.

Finally, to clear her mind and get a better perspective, she removed her clothes. She stood naked under the cold shower, forcing life back into her body and shivered with the sting of the water.

After midnight she finally lay down on the bed in her pajamas. It was a hot, sultry night and in no time at all, her sheet and pillows were damp. She kicked off her pajama bottoms, but that did not help. In a few minutes she took off the top. Even naked, she could not find sleep or comfort in her bedroom.

At one-thirty in the morning, she arose. The room had grown oppressive and she pulled on a thin robe, lit a cigarette and walked through the clubhouse. She sat down on a motor crate that belonged to one of her customers and looked at the river. It was dark and forbidding. Far down the bend she saw the red and green running lights of a coal barge tow. The tireless blinking of a navigation light on the far tip of the island on the Illinois side winked back at her in a steady rhythm. In time she controlled her heartache. Her initial disappointment in Monte wore off and her thoughts became more logical. What horrified her most was her own reaction. Until now she had not realized how much she cared for him. In a very short time she had fallen "head over heels" in love with Monte. Now, that love must give way to more practical considerations. For a few minutes, tears blinded her eyes. In silence they pushed over the rims of her eyelids and rolled down her cheeks. With the tears gone, she merely sat there as if suspended in time and space.

"What's the matter, Cap'n?" Matt's voice come out of the darkness. The old man had been sleeping down in the boatshed but had decided because of the heat to move up under one of the remaining elms that had not been destroyed by the dreaded Dutch-elm disease that was sweeping across the countryside.

"Too hot for you?"

"Yes, I guess that's it, Matt."

"I've been in the boatshed. Plenty hot there. I'm going to sleep out in the open for a while." He moved on and settled himself a few yards away from her.

In no time, Carol heard a soft snore. She swatted at a mosquito around her ear but missed. She sighed and stood up. There was nothing to be gained by sitting here any longer. Physical and emotional weariness overcame her. She returned to her room and lay down on the bed. Even then, the first false light of dawn spread over the eastern sky before she dropped off to sleep. With the dawn came the cool breeze. It drifted up from the riverbank and fluttered the curtains, then curled its way into her restless sleep and made a soft message soft, *What now?*

Though she fought to keep the drug of slumber, Carol awoke just a few hours later. She was worn out but further rest was impossible. Her leg muscles ached when she arose. Every fiber of her body was stiff and sore. The world was devoid of all hope and cheer. Like a robot, she got into her shorts and halter, positioned the yachting cap on the back of her head and went to the lunch counter to fix herself some black coffee.

She came back to life slowly. Matt was down on the dock, putting out anchor lines so that the docks would not be grounded as the river continued to fall. The milkman drove over from Riverview, filled his eyes with her image and left the day's supply. The coffee jarred Carol's nerves.

For a while Carol considered the possibility that Joe had made up the story about Monte. She examined it from every angle because she did not want to believe it, but Joe was too unimaginative to dream up a thing like that. No way was he fool enough to think she would be taken in by such a story for long. No, Joe was right. It was Monte Abbott who was wrong.

A flame of resentment toward Monte caught fire within her. It fed on well-prepared tinder, and as she began the day's routine it flared ever higher. In time, Carol was consumed with a white-hot anger for the man who had caused her such disappointment and chagrin.

The sky was overcast all morning, and in the afternoon a light rain began to fall. Activity came to a stop on the dock. No one went out on the river in this kind of weather unless he had to. Carol worked in the clubhouse to complete an inventory as a thunderstorm brewed into the evening.

Wally slouched behind the lunch counter with a magazine in his lap, waiting for six o'clock to fix dinner for both of them. Afterwards, Carol said he might as well take off for the evening. There would be no customers around, due to the bad storm.

Persistent work and make busy tasks spared Carol the torture of thinking about Monte. In her room as the rain drops pounded on the roof, she tried to loose herself in a book. She almost succeeded when around nine o'clock Monte knocked at her door and entered her room. He had just gotten back from town.

He took off his raincoat and grinned. "I don't think the rain is going to bother us, do you?"

Carol looked at him. The anger and resentment that had burned in her all day rose close to the surface, but she held herself in check. She wanted to handle this with care.

"No reason why it should," she said flatly.

He came over and kissed her. She stood stiffly. He stepped back and smiled, "Is anything wrong, Carol?"

"There's been something wrong the whole time I've known you."

He frowned. "I don't get it."

"Can't you guess?" she asked – the words were slow and with contempt.

"Why, no." Alarm spread through his eyes. "What is it?"

"I didn't know until last night what a heel you are." she stormed.

"Carol."

"You didn't tell me you were married. You kept that a secret. You didn't want to spoil your fun."

He stared in awe and admiration. Carol was gorgeous to look at, but with fury raging across her attractive features, she was breathtaking. "You've got to let me explain, Carol," he faltered.

"You can get the hell out of here. And take your boat with you. You lied and cheated from the minute we met."

"I can explain that."

"I don't want any explanation. Get out." she cried

Monte looked grim. She was being unreasonable. "Sure, I'm married –but that's not the whole story. I haven't lived with my wife for six months. That's why I came to St. Louis."

"Get out. I won't listen."

"You will listen." he shouted back at her.

His outburst surprised her. His jaw was set, and determination was in his eyes. She measured him carefully and decided it was best to let him speak his side of the story.

"At least, I won't have to believe what I hear from you," she said with disdain in her voice. She plopped down and crossed her arms.

Monte gave a despairing look, but determined to have his say; he walked around in front of her. "Hadley left me—"

"So that's her name. All the time I was on your boat, you had her name right up there for everybody to see."

"I can't help that, Carol. The boat was named over a year ago. Anyway, she left me because she thought I spent too much time on the river. She likes high society living, dressing up, parties, formalities. And I hate it. Give me a stretch of water, some sun and a good boat to a fancy dinner party any day. But that's not for Hadley."

"We were married two years ago," he continued slowly, "six months ago she left me. She's a St. Louis girl, and that's why I came here. I wanted to get our marriage settled one way or the other. When I met you I knew what way I wanted it settled."

She gave him a look of disbelief. Monte went on, "I've been trying since I got here to get her to ask for a divorce, but she won't say what she wants. All she knows is that she wants me to give up boating as my hobby and exchange all my slacks for tuxedos. Just yesterday I told her I'd never do that."

"Do you think I'm interested in your domestic troubles?" Carol asked thinly. "You lied to me. That's all that matters."

"I never lied to you. I just never said anything about being married. Maybe I was wrong in that but I had a reason. I wanted to know where I stood. I wanted to be able to tell you that I'd soon be free, and you and I could—" He paused and made a helpless gesture – "Well, work out something."

"If you're through now, you can leave."

"Don't you believe me?"

"I wouldn't believe anything you said."

Monte studied her. He sensed how distraught she was, but he was more taken than ever with her beauty. He felt drawn to her and realized he loved her more than life. He knew it for a certainty now.

"I want to marry you, Carol—if I ever can."

"You're pretty safe in saying that, when your wife won't let you go."

"Damn it, if she won't divorce me, I'll divorce her. I've already said that. I've talked to a lawyer."

"When you're through talking, get out."

Carol picked up a cigarette. Her hands shook as she lit it. She walked to the other side of the room and stood by a window. Tears for being so gullible welled up. The pelting rain against the window matched her mood.

Monte came over to her. "I've told you the truth. You don't have to believe it, but you know everything now."

"Why did you try to hide it? If I hadn't found out, you'd have gone right on letting me think you were honest."

"It wasn't that," he said distressed. "I wasn't trying to fool you. I wanted to reach a settlement with Hadley before I told you."

Carol moved away from him. He caught her by her arm and turned her around, searching her eyes for some glimmer that she believed him. All he saw was contempt. She blew smoke into his face.

Monte gave in to a sudden, wild desire. He crushed her to him and forced his lips on hers. It happened so quickly that she was stunned, but rebellion flooded her. She tried to push him away, but could not budge him. Frustration added fuel to her fury. She broke away, for a second, then he caught her, and they fell against the couch.

Their emotions, raw from the strain of the last few minutes, found sudden release in physical exertion. Monte was determined to pierce her icy reserve, and Carol was just as determined that he would not. She fought like a wildcat, but his strength was too much for her. She was down, but not subdued. She bent her knees in a frenzied effort to get free. She used her legs to leverage against him. She exerted every ounce of her power, but it was not enough. A sob escaped as her resistance was broken.

Monte's mouth was like fire on hers. He made no attempt to hold his passion in check. Carol was overwhelmed. His desire made a wreck of her anger and hatred. Though her mind rejected him, her body responded to his desire. With ragged breath she grabbed his right hand and nibbled on each finger tip. She slowly pushed his middle finger deep into her mouth and sucked it.

The distant throaty bass whistles of a riverboat vibrated the still night air. A locust on the river bank gave two ratchet-like, swelling signals that dwindled back into silence. Carol took a deep breath, drinking into her lungs the tangy, humid odor of the river. The thunderstorm had passed.

Monte stirred in response to her movement. "I love you, so very much, Carol," he murmured in her ear.

She did not say anything. Her future, long in doubt, was more unsettled than ever. She tried to swallow her grief, but it would not stay down. The sobs that followed were beyond consolation. The one she loved belonged to somebody else.

8 Frank Postponed

Events had forced a shift in Carol's attitude toward Frank Weaver. She could not afford to lose the Cabaret Boat Dock right now – her mission to preserve Cabaret Island for wildlife and prevent any takeover by outside investors consumed her thoughts. Means had to be found to stall Frank for another week, maybe a month or even longer. Her operating capital was down to practically nothing. She needed some cash badly.

The only solution she could come up with, after an hour of work at her desk the following morning, was to try to negotiate a loan on some of her equipment. That would put her even deeper into debt, but she could think of nothing else to do.

She made a call to her bank in St. Louis and inquired about the possibility of getting a loan. Michael Lutz was receptive and asked if she could get into town by noon. Carol agreed and hung up.

She went to the dock to tell Matt that she would be gone part of the day. He was sitting in the work skiff at the stern of Monte's cruiser, scraping the mahogany hull with a large putty knife.

"What's going on, Matt?" she called over to him.

"Mr. Abbot asked me to take the name off his boat. He doesn't want to call it *Hadley* anymore."

She considered the significance of that. Not a bad omen, but she dare not let it build up her hopes. Monte was a married man.

He might remain married a long time. Changing the name of his boat could mean very little.

"Is Mr. Abbott around?" she asked.

"No, he left early this morning. Said he was going to town on business."

She wondered what that business might be about as she went back to the clubhouse. She had a feeling it might be in connection with his wife. He might be getting ready to force the woman to give him his freedom.

Carol caught herself gloating over the possibility. She was shocked by her own attitude and quickly put it from her mind. What he did was his own business. She wanted no part of disrupting someone else's marriage.

What had happened last night had not changed her mind. The accusation she had made against him still stood. Monte had been wrong in not telling her the truth. She was torn between that feeling and the deep yearning she felt for him.

Carole slipped into a business-style frock and black pumps and drove into St Louis in the station wagon. She went to the bank and spent an hour with Mr. Lutz, an understanding, middle-aged man who had handled several financial deals for her father a number of years ago. She left with a loan of one thousand dollars.

At two o'clock she walked into Frank Weaver's office on the fourth floor of a downtown office building. It was a single-suite office from which Frank managed the Ebbs Estate. He leaped up from behind his desk when she entered. Surprise and pleasure crossed his face at the sight of her. "Well, Carol." he exclaimed. "I'm honored by your visit. Sit down."

He pulled a chair around for her beside the desk. She sat down and mounted one knee upon the other. Frank leaned back in his chair and surveyed her with anticipation. He much preferred her in the shorts and halter top that she wore around the docks, but she was enticing in a dress as well.

"I've decided to do something about the loan, Frank," she told him, careful to hold her animosity in check.

Anticipation leaped into his eyes for a second. "I'm awfully glad you have, Carol. I'm the last one to want to see you lose out."

She forced a smile. If he felt that way, it was only because he might lose his position of influence with her.

Frank sat forward in his chair. His voice was low and intimate. "I can handle the trustees. Don't worry about that one minute. Sooner or later, of course, you'll have to pay something on the loan, but for now I can hold them off. Just forget about it. Meanwhile, what do you say we have dinner together tonight?"

"I came to make a payment on the loan," she informed him.

Frank's face fell. Then he reconsidered her words and brightened. "I know, but we'll want to make an evening of it. After all-"

"You were right the first time," Carol said. "This isn't going to be the sort of payment you're after."

"You mean-?"

"Will one thousand dollars make you leave me alone?"

"You brought money?" It was hard for him to believe. He knew how hard-pressed she had been.

"What else?"

"Naturally we will be glad to accept any money you can pay," Frank said.

Once again Carol Burke proved too elusive for him. He made an effort to regain his dignity, but failed to hide his disappointment.

"Then here is one thousand dollars. I'd like a receipt for it, please," she said.

"Yes, of course."

Frank stared glumly at the check she placed on the desk before him. Her smile was cryptic. He looked at her. Frank felt cheated but there was nothing to do but write her out a receipt.

"I'm glad you were able to do this, Carol," he said handing it to her.

"I'll bet you are." She shot back, unable to conceal her contempt any longer. "You didn't want me to pay anything. Not this way. Who do you think you're kidding—outside of the trustee?"

"Don't forget there'll be more payments to make," he said, dropping all pretenses. "Will you be able to raise the money each time?"

 "That's my worry, isn't it?

"It doesn't have to be," he told her.

"When I get charitable with you, you'll know I'm pretty damned hard up."

With that Carol turned and marched out of the office. She had lost her temper with him in spite of everything. She had not intended to. The time may come when she would not have the money to hold him off, and other means might be called for. Well, she would have to cross that bridge when she came to it. For now, she had managed to keep one wolf from her door.

Monte's Cadillac was parked near the clubhouse when Carol returned late that afternoon. She put the receipt she had gotten from Frank in her desk then went to the dock to check her supply of gasoline at the pump. Monte waved to her from his cruiser. When she finished at the pump, he called her over.

"How do you like it?" he said, pointing toward the stern of his boat.

Carol stared. He had painted a new name where the old one had been. It was *CAROL*. At first she was pleased, but further thought tempered her reaction.

"You're reaching pretty far out to make an impression, Monte."

"Maybe that isn't as important as getting the first name off. Can you come aboard for a minute?"

Carol hesitated. She had no business going aboard his boat. She was out to see as little of him as possible, but that was asking too much of her heart. She stepped into the boat and sat down in the cockpit.

"I had a long meeting with my lawyer this morning," Monte began. "He isn't very encouraging about my chances of getting a divorce, unless Hadley agrees to it."

"That's none of my affair."

Monte gave her a vindictive look. "You're right. Of course, but I wanted you to know what I'm trying to do. My lawyer promised to get in touch with her this afternoon."

"That doesn't change things. You still weren't honest with me when we first met."

"I didn't know I'd fall in love with you," he said.

Carol looked across the river. The water was bright in the late afternoon sun. The sandbar on the Illinois shore was dazzling white. Beyond it, the willows that lined the river bank made a curtain of deep green between the sky and the horizon. Cabaret Island lay unprotected – like a virgin. She thought of last night, and of the night she had come to his boat. They were thoughts that awakened memories of passion shared.

"I'll never be happy until I can have you as my own," he said huskily – moving closer to her.

She felt his hand on her arm. It sent a magic tremor vibrating from her lips to her burning groin and back again. She fought against the yearning he aroused. She was about to pull away from him when footsteps sounded on the dock beside the boat.

A cold, haughty voice broke in on them. "So this is the reason."

Carol looked up. A tall, slender, blond woman, in an expensive light, summer dress, stood on the dock. Her blue eyes looked down at them with a combination of fire and ice. Monte leaped to his feet. "Hello, Hadley," he stammered. "Er---this is Miss Carol Burke. She runs the boat dock."

"From the look of things, she runs the men who dock here too." Hadley's voice was acid. She looked Carol up and down, plainly disdainful of what she saw.

The woman's attitude infuriated Carol, but she could think of no reply. Before she could move, Hadley stepped aboard the cruiser and faced Monte.

"What was the idea of sending a lawyer out to see me?" Hadley demanded with anger.

"Didn't he explain?" Monte asked.

"You bet he did and I told him off. Why didn't you come yourself? Are you afraid to leave this river trash…. Did you invite her aboard?"

"Now listen, Hadley, we've been over all of this before."

"You've got some nerve thinking you can pull something like that on me." Hadley told him emphatically. She turned her back to Carol as if the angry river girl did not exist.

"Well, I'm willing to let you get the divorce. I told you that," Monte said.

Carol decided to leave them alone. This was no place for her. She stepped over to the dock. She was about to walk away when Hadley' contemptuous words came to her. "Is she the one?"

"Yes," Monte replied.

Carol stopped. She turned around and gave Hadley a deadly look. Still there was nothing she could say. This man and woman were husband and wife. She had no right to participate in their argument. Carol's angry look did not sit well with Hadley. The stately blonde laughed with contempt at the river girl.

"It's no fun being married to a boat lover," said Hadley. "But if you think I'm going to hand him to you or anybody else on a silver platter, you're crazy."

Carol stormed off. She was afraid that if she remained there another second she would strike the haughty, high-class shrew. Carol could not help feeling sorry for Monte, married to such a vicious, spiteful snob. As Carol approached the clubhouse she noticed a smart looking cream-colored, leather-upholstered convertible parked nearby. *Hadley's no doubt.*

Forty minutes later, Hadley and Monte came up from the dock. Carol watched from the clubhouse as Hadley walked to her convertible. Monte stood with his hands in his pockets until she drove off. He came into the clubhouse. Carol rushed to her desk. She did not want him to think she had been eavesdropping. "She won't listen to reason," he said shaking his head.

"Not going to let you go. Is that it?"

"Not without certain considerations, which I can't possibly meet."

"What then?"

"She doesn't want me back. All she wants me to do is supply her with money, and she doesn't even need it. She has plenty of her own."

"Why should she be so ornery then?" Carol asked. "Have you always been honest with her, or did you deal with her like you did with me?"

He gave her a reproachful glance. "Be careful, Carol. Can't you see how sorry I am for not telling you I was married?"

Just then Matt came in. He needed direction on a job he was doing down at the boatshed. Carol went with him. It took her twenty minutes to get Matt straightened out, and when she returned to the clubhouse Monte was gone.

Early that evening Joe Mosley called. He had a night off and wanted Carol to have a beer with him. She didn't care to, but she was afraid if she remained around the clubhouse she might end up with Monte. That would only make matters worse between them. The sooner she overcame her desire for him, the better off she would be.

"Okay," she said.

"Sounds like you're beginning to come to your senses," Joe chuckled over the telephone.

"If you're going to be rubbing it in, we'll just call the date off right now." Carol snapped.

"Naw, kidding. I was just kidding," said Joe. "See you at eight, baby."

Carol slammed down the telephone. She wished she had not made the date with Joe, but it was too late now. He would come for her at eight. Five minutes later, Monte came up from his boat and entered the clubhouse.

"Let's go some place for dinner, Carol," he said.

"Sorry, but I've made other arrangements."

He stared at her. She saw the hurt and disappointment in his eyes, and it was like a knife in her heart. He gave her a faint smile.

"Okay," he said. "I sure can't expect you to keep your evenings open for me. I've got no right to ask you for anything while I'm married."

Monte's shoulders sagged as he walked out. She fought an impulse to run after him and say she was sorry, to tell him she had not meant a word she had said. She wanted to erase the cares of the world from his tired features, but she held back bitterly. Her heart was left with an empty ache.

The evening with Joe loomed ahead of her, stupid and meaningless. The wind pushed the curtains and slammed the screen door shut. *What are you going to do?*

Tears welled up as she turned to her bedroom.

9 Disaster on the Mississippi

Schwartz's, where Joe took her that evening, was a river man's hangout. It sat near the levee north of Eads Bridge, a nondescript-looking place, wedged in between two large and dark warehouses. But it was a first-class place to eat and drink, well-known to all river men on the upper Mississippi. Carol had not been there in several months, and Schwartz, a huge, mild-manner tavern operator, came over to the booth where she and Joe sat to greet them and as *"Hello - how are things going?"* came out of his mouth, Carol began looking around.

Carol saw others she knew. Ralph Stark, chief engineer on the excursion boat, St Louis Belle, John Wade of the harbor master's office and big Harry Wilson, a towboat captain from Cairo. There was also Oren Brooks, first mate on a Missouri Valley Barge Line towboat, who had dated Carol a few times last year.

They were men who carried the traditions of a river, long since removed from the glamour of bygone days. Yet, they moved more tonnage up and down its winding, yellow course than had ever been dreamed of by the masters of the Lee and the Natchez. With their snub-nosed, twin-screw, diesel-powered towboats, they pushed heavily-laden barges up the crest of the current carrying oil, coal and other cargoes to the cities of the north. These men knew the river as their predecessors had but they also knew how to set up an approach to each lock and the charts of the nine-foot channel by heart. They spoke the parlance of ship-to-shore radio telephones, and were veterans in the use of radar to avoid disaster in the treacherous stretches of the river and keep an easy distance off shore.

Carol had grown up with these people. She knew their language, their dislikes and loyalties. She shared their interest in the river as a livelihood and knew the meaning of low water and floods. Their heritage was hers. They were river men and she, a river girl.

She did not think about all of this as she and Joe Mosley sat in Schwartz's talking and drinking beer that evening, it was simply a part of her. Instead, she thought of her evening with Monte on the Chase Hotel roof. Carol sat back and felt more in control here.

The sights and sounds were more familiar, the faces more distinct and clear. This was no place of high fashion and champagne cocktails. It was a place of river men in loose jackets and beer. Over it all, the pungent, omnipresent odor of the river, with its cocktail of mud and fish, rolled forever southward with majestic indifference to man.

"Like old times again," Joe said. "You and me sitting around having ourselves some fun." He pressed his knee against hers under the table.

"I guess it is," she shrugged and pulled in her leg.

"I hope you're straightened out about that Abbott guy by now."

"I wouldn't know."

"What did he say when you told him you knew about his wife?"

Carol remembered the stormy scene for a moment. Then she looked with irritation at Joe, "Do we have to talk about that?"

"No," he smiled, "I was just asking."

Joe kept up a constant stream of chatter. Mrs. Hattie Blackburn joined them in the booth and Joe was bothered with her interruption, but Carol smiled at the woman's friendly greeting. Hattie was married to old Pete Blackburn, who had been on the river with her father. She was near seventy, hawk-nosed, but had a twinkle in her eyes and the energy of a much younger woman.

"How 'ave you been, dearie? Haven't seen you around here for a spell," said Hattie, pleased to see Carol again.

"I've been pretty busy."

"I know you are. My, but you're a grand girl, carrying on up on those docks just like your father. Takes nerve, believe me. Is Joe helping you?" She asked, gesturing toward him.

"Some," Carol replied to make conversation.

Hattie gave Joe a look of disapproval. She had known him a long time. "You're going to be just like the rest. I swear, river men are all the same whether they're old or young. Take Pete, for instance, he told me to be here at nine o'clock. Well, it's going on eleven and he hasn't showed yet. That's a river man for you."

"I got up to Carol's on time, Hattie. Ask her if you don't believe me," said Joe for his own behalf.

"Pete did too, when he was courtin' me." Hattie shot Carol a smile and a wink. "But the minute he knew he was safe, he quit that. Hasn't been on time since. Why I've waited not hours, but days, for that man. I'll never forget-"

Hattie launched into a long rambling story which soon strayed from the original point and turned into a condemnation of river men and the lives they led. Marriage to a river man, Hattie pointed out was a half marriage. At the end of a year, Pete had been home only half the time.

Carol could remember her father's cousin talking like that, too. Cousin Mary said that Carol's mother had complained of knowing Sam Burke only in snatches. Home for a few nights or a week. Then off again on a 28-day hitch to Memphis, Vicksburg, or Louisville.

"If you're thinking of snagging your fate to this young river man, just remember dearie, that you'll be keeping dinner hot for him when he's nowhere near. And he'll bust in home for a week's stay when you figure he's down on the Ohio," Hattie concluded.

The old woman laughed raucously. She enjoyed life, even though she spoke as if it was her despair. In her youth, Hattie had spent few lonely nights when Pete was away. If Pete had heard the *Blues on Basin Street* in his younger days, traveling to the red-light district of the New Orleans French Quarter, it was a cinch that Hattie was in no position to play the role of an outraged wife.

Hattie had earned extra cash at the brothel approved by the Health Department to operate near St. Louis City Hall in the 1920's and the *Red Rooster's* madam on Washington Street in the 1930's welcomed Hattie's services. Life was not going to catch her waiting at home.

"There's your guy now," said Joe dryly.

Hattie looked around as a stoop-shouldered old man entered Schwartz's. Hattie jumped up.

"I enjoyed the visit with you two young folks," she said but bustled off to join her husband who gave her a courtly bow, but said nothing as they went to a table.

Carol's eyes had followed Hattie Blackburn as she left the booth. She realized that in looking at Hattie she might be looking at herself, fifty years from now. A shudder ran down her spine.

The walls of Schwartz's seemed to press in on Carol. She thought of Monte and the world he represented, a world that stretched far back from the river banks, a modern world confined to no valley, a world she had seen on numerous occasions and which she knew existed for others. Her world of the river was something else again. In a sudden moment of despondency it seemed to her that she would never escape it. Monte was married. *Was Joe Mosley her fate?*

"How about another beer?" he said.

"Make mine a whiskey. Straight," said Carol.

Joe's eyebrows shot up. He gaped at her in astonishment. "Whiskey? On top of all the beer we've had?"

"That's what I said."

Seward Jenkins, the waiter, came over. Joe ordered a whiskey for Carol and another beer for himself. Seward looked at Joe to see if he had heard right. Joe nodded. Seward picked up their empty glasses, hesitated, then shrugged as he hurried away.

"What's the idea?" asked Joe looking at her sternly. "I never knew you to switch to whiskey this late in the evening."

"I'm tired of beer. Isn't that reason enough?" she glared at him with defiance.

"I guess it is, but don't blame me if you get boiled."

Carol contemplated the jigger of whiskey the waiter placed before her. Then she downed it in one gulp and followed it with a water chase. Joe watched the performance and shook his head. He had difficulty understanding her at times. She had two more and her thoughts grew fuzzy.

"Let's get out of here," she said abruptly.

"What's the matter with Schwartz'?"

"Nothing, I'm just tired of it. Come on. Move." She pushed against Joe's arm so she could get out of the booth.

They visited another river tavern on the landing. Carol downed a few more straight whiskeys. She reached a state where her mind and senses were dulled. Nothing seemed to matter. Time did not exist. Space was elongated out of proportion. Nothing was quite right, but it made no difference.

At a quarter of two in the morning, Carol and Joe stood on the cobblestone pavement in an old section of St. Louis on the landing, near the warehouses by the river. Joe had gotten drunk in an effort to keep up with her. He swayed as he fumbled for the keys to his car.

"That's funny," he muttered.

"What's funny?"

"No keys."

Arm-in-arm they staggered back to the last tavern. The proprietor was closing up. When they asked if he had seen Joe's keys, he had not. Besides, he was tired and anxious to get home. To get rid of them, he set them up to a drink apiece, then ushered them good-naturedly out of his place. They swayed back to the car. They would never get home without keys.

Through the fog, Carol's brain blindly headed for home. "Let's go up the river," she suggested.

Joe thought she had lost her mind. "Better yet, let's fly."

"No, let's go borrow one of Bill Raft's speed boats."

Joe admired her resourcefulness. "I never would've thought of it," he declared.

They stumbled down to the levee. Bill Raft operated a couple of speed boats from a small dock, taking sight seers on trips around the harbor in the afternoons and evening. Raft's place was closed, but they awakened Slim Carter, the caretaker who slept on a small cot in the office. Slim stared as they told him the purpose of their visit.

"But I can't let you take a boat at this hour," he said.

"Aw, sure you can. I've got to run Carol up to the Cabaret Dock. I'll be back in an hour and Bill won't ever know the difference."

"But what if something happens?"

"You think we're going to let anything happen, a couple of old river rats like Joe and me?" Carol laughed.

Joe forced a ten-dollar bill into Slim's hand to convince the caretaker. He untied one of the speedboats. Joe steadied himself behind the wheel and Carol tumbled in beside him. With a cheerful wave to Bill, Joe started the motor and pushed the accelerator into high speed at the same time.

The speedboat roared out into the river, the bow rising out of the water. He pulled the wheel hard to port, and the boat headed upstream. In less practiced hands, such a venture would have been too risky, but Joe and Carol responded gaily to the wind and the spray as the boat raced through the night, under the bridges past the humming powerhouse and the lighted docks of the St Louis Terminal.

Beyond the harbor they moved in inky darkness, guided only by the familiar blinking of the lights and landmarks. For the first few minutes, Carol felt a dim exhilaration shoot through her dulled senses. Then she eased back against the leather cushion. She was asleep when Joe throttled down the engine and maneuvered into the Cabaret Dock an hour later.

A short while before, Monte had awakened in his bunk, aboard the cruiser. Unable to get back to sleep – he had brought his thoughts of Carol with him as he put his feet in his slippers and walked back to the cockpit where he sat, smoking a pipe and contemplating the river. He heard an approaching speedboat from far down the river, but not until it neared the docks, did he pay any attention to it. He could see its red and green running lights across the water. When the motor throttled, he knew it was headed toward Cabaret dock. He stood up and looked toward the lights with idle curiosity.

One dim night light showed on the dock. The speedboat came up to it and drifted against the dockside. Joe Mosley got out. He stumbled but recovered and managed to attach the boat to a wooden cleat. He swayed unsteadily then got back in the boat, lifted Carol into his arms and returned to the dock. The wake, kicked up by the speedboat, began to make the dock rock. Joe staggered around – precariously.

Monte had witnessed all of this with slow surprise and wonder, but now he was shot through with fear. *Had something happened to Carol?* Joe held her in his arms and tottered around as if he might plunge them both in the river. Monte headed to the dock and ran along the planks.

"What's the matter?" he asked.

Joe looked around and did not see who it was. When he recognized Monte, he growled, "Nothing's the matter. Mind your own damned business."

"But what's wrong with Carol?"

"She passed out. Now get away, do you hear?" With that Joe started along the dock.

"Look out." Monte cried as Joe teetered near the edge.

Monte sprang forward and pulled Joe to safety. Joe glared. He tried to shake free of Monte's grasp, but with Carol in his arms he had no success.

"Let go of me," Joe growled.

"You're drunk. You'd better put her down before you both fall in the river," said Monte.

"Don't tell me what to do."

Monte was too concerned with Carol's safety to humor Joe. He stared at the river man – his words were crisp.

"I said, put her down."

Joe stood Carol on her feet. The two men shoved each other. Carol was jarred awake. She had no idea where she was. She heard heated words and looked around to see what was going on. It got through to her that Monte and Joe were squaring off. She walked toward them and stepped off into emptiness. Carol hit the water with a splash.

The cold current dragged Carol under. She kicked frantically to the surface. The splash she made stopped the fight between Joe and Monte. Both men stared toward the water. Carol had been swept halfway to the end of the dock by the time she came up. She sobered in an instant and swam with all of her strength toward the dock. Just as she reached out to grab hold, she was carried beyond its southernmost tip.

She let out a yell for help and both men jumped into the speedboat. Carol knew this part of the river. She was in a dangerous current but she was a good swimmer. She unfastened her skirt, kicked out of it, then headed for the bank. A dike protruded from the shore a considerable distance below the dock, and she had to make it to safety before the current carried her into it. The most expert swimmer in the world could not overcome the sucking force of the water against the dike.

Her lungs pumped air and her heart pounded like a sledge-hammer when she pulled herself onto the river bank. She lay exhausted. After a time she sat up and looked toward the river. The speedboat made circles, its light sweeping the water. She got to her feet and waved her arms. Even if she could have yelled her lungs out, she would never make herself heard over the roar of the motor. The light swept the bank a couple of times but missed her. They could never see her in this darkness.

To her horror, the boat swept in a wide arc above the dike. It turned away from the bank and shot toward open water. Whoever was at the wheel misjudged his distance, and the boat snagged an end piling. There was a sharp, cranking sound. The motor went dead, and the running lights went out.

What a nightmare. Carol started running back toward the clubhouse. She fought and stumbled through underbrush and over rocks, slipping and falling several times in the mud.

The current had carried her quite a way down the river. She thought she would never make it back. It was taking forever. Finally, she staggered into the light which Matt had turned on at the club house. He ran to her from the dock, his eyes wide with fear.

"What's happened, Cap'n?" he gasped. She did not answer. Instead she started toward the clubhouse but fell from exhaustion. Matt picked her up and helped her inside.

"Call the Coast Guard right away, Matt," she gasped.

Then Carol collapsed.

10   Carol gets Nasty

The terror of the previous night poured in on Carol's brain the instant she awoke. She bolted to a sitting position on her bed. It was still early but light. In less than two minutes she had slipped into her shorts, halter and deck shoes and left her bedroom. The clubhouse was deserted, but several cars were parked outside. A number of men were grouped about in serious talk. Joe was there, but not Monte.

"Where's Monte?" she cried, running to them.

"He went down to his boat for a few minutes, Cap'n," Matt told her. "He'll be right back."

"Then he's safe?"

"Yes."

Carol uttered a silent prayer of gratitude. She looked around. Bill Raft was there, highly perturbed over who was going to pay for the damage to his boat. No one paid any attention to him. The others present included several men from the Coast Guard, a newspaper reporter, a photographer, and two policemen.

The newspaper reporter began asking Carol questions. Of necessity, her account of the night's events was halting and unsure.

She had not yet had time to straighten things out in her mind, but what she said satisfied the reporter who had a deadline to make.

Monte then came up the stairs from the dock. He looked haggard but otherwise intact.

"Now how about a picture of the three of you?" asked the reporter.

Before anybody could answer he motioned for the photographer.

The photographer, a cynical individual who had photographed presidents and juvenile delinquents with equal disregard, began issuing orders. Against the will of all three, he lined Monte, Carol and Joe up for a picture. He took one look at Carol's legs and backed up for a full-length shot. The flash bulb went off, and within a few moments, the reporter and photographer took off in a car for St. Louis.

"We've got to get statements from you in order to complete our report," said one of the policemen to Carol. "How did you happen to fall into the river last night?"

"I don't know, I just did," she replied.

"Was it dark down there on the dock?"

"I explained all of that, Officer," Monte spoke up. "She was asleep and----"

"Shut up. I want to get her side of the story," said the policeman.

"No, it wasn't dark completely. I always leave a light on."

"You own this dock, don't you?"

"Yes."

"You weren't pushed into the river or anything?" asked the policeman.

"No."

"How about the speedboat? How come you and this fellow, Mosley, were cavorting around in the middle of the night on a boat that didn't belong to you?"

"Joe borrowed it to bring me home. He'd lost the keys to his car."

"Borrowed it?" the officer asked wryly.

"You don't think we'd steal it, do you?' Carol snapped.

Bill Raft spoke up at that point. "Look, I wasn't accusing Joe and Carol of stealing the boat, officer. They just took it, see? They're friends of mine. All I'm interested in is finding out who's going to pay the damage."

"Ask him," said Joe pointing to Monte. "He was at the wheel when we slammed into the dike."

"You're the one who took the boat," Monte cut in. "I relieved you at the wheel because you wanted to work the searchlight when we were trying to find Carol."

Everyone started talking at once. There were threats, accusations, and denials. The two policemen listened helplessly for a few minutes. Then the one who had been doing the interrogating raised his voice.

"Quiet." he shouted. "We ain't getting anywhere with this."

He turned to Raft. "Now, look. It's your boat that was wrecked. What do you want to do, have these people arrested or not?"

"I don't want them arrested, but I want to know who's going to pay the damages."

"If you don't want us to arrest them, there's nothing further we can do. You'd better get a lawyer and sue them." The officer turned to his companion, "Come on, Adam, let's get out of this bughouse."

The police drove away in their patrol car. Bill Raft looked at Monte and Joe. He was a thin-framed man with mechanics' hands and a smile. His blue eyes had turned bitter. "Well, how about it? Do I have to lose out because one of you borrowed my boat and the other one hung it on a dike?"

"Haven't you got insurance, Bill?" Carol asked.

"No. you know how expensive those marine policies are."

Exhausted, Monte plopped down on a coil of rope. "I don't think I'm to blame, but when you find out how much the damage runs, I'll pay half. I'm damned, though, if I'm going to be stuck for the whole repair bill."

Joe listened to this offer in sullen silence. He was unwilling to shoulder any blame when he was not at the wheel. That was how responsibility was fixed on the river, and he stubbornly refused to admit any personal liability beyond that.

"How about you, Carol?" Raft asked. "You were in on this thing. How about you kickin' in some?"

She looked away in despair. She felt obligated. If she had not fallen in the river, the boat never would have been wrecked, but how could she help pay for repairs when she was already head over heels in debt?

"Why don't you get an estimate of the damage, Bill?" she suggested. It was the only thing she could think of to say. "When we know how much money is involved, we can talk about it further. I agree you oughtn't to lose out on our account."

Raft was far from satisfied, but he could get no further commitment from any of them. He walked to his car to drive back into town, and since Joe had to get back to his job, he got into Bill's car. With those arrangements made, Joe and Bill drove off, and Matt wandered off.

The Coast Guard men left a few minutes later, towing Bill's boat down to the harbor at St Louis' landing, as they had agreed. Carol and Monte were left alone.

"At least you got out alive," Monte remarked.

She looked down at him. "How did you get mixed up in it in the first place?'

"I saw you and Joe come in last night. I was awake and sitting on my boat. You were both so drunk you didn't know what you were doing. I merely tried to keep you from getting drowned."

"It might have been better if I had," she said.

"Why did you get soused with him?"

"I've got a right to do that."

"Sure you have, but—"

"At least Joe isn't married. And if he was, I think he'd have the decency to tell me."

She marched into the clubhouse where Wally had her breakfast ready. She sat down and was half-finished when Monte came in. He ordered a cup of coffee and the silence filled the room.

Reflecting back on last night, Carol became more depressed than ever. She thought of Hattie, of Joe and of river men in general, and then she thought of Monte. She and he were worlds apart, and from the looks of things they would remain that way.

"I'm going into town today and talk with my lawyer's partner in St Louis again," offered Monte.

"Is that so?" Her tone was indifferent.

"If there's a chance I can get my freedom, would you consider me at all, Carol?" he asked.

"Let's face it, Monte. You're not used to my sort of life—and I'm not used to yours."

"I'm not interested in my kind of life. I've always been more interested in the river, and now I'm interested in you. Won't you please think it over?" he said huskily.

"I don't know what good it's going to do," she said. "You're still married, and from the looks of things you're going to stay that way."

"I am not." he retorted. "Hadley and I haven't ever gotten along. I'm going to make her see that."

Carol sipped her coffee. "That's your business. Not mine."

Monte left and Carol slumped at the counter a while longer, gathering her strength to get through the day. There was much to be done. It could not wait, just because she was worn out from the hectic events of last night. She had to keep going, if not for herself, then for her creditors. With a sigh, she pushed herself up and went to work.

The day was drudgery. Matters got worse when Wally came back from Baden with an afternoon paper. He showed her an item of interest on page three. There was the two-column photo of Monte, Joe and Carol. An account of her fall into the Mississippi River, the ensuing attempt at rescue by Monte and Joe, ending with the wreck of Bill Raft's speedboat to round out the article.

As Carol read the account, she knew this would not help the Cabaret Boat Dock. Such goings-on made the dock look like a honky-tonk place where anything could happen and boats were not safe. A boat owner would think twice before patronizing her.

"That's just dandy," she said, handing the paper back.

"But you got your name in the paper," he said.

"That sort of publicity won't help. I'm not running a sideshow."

Carol picked up the binoculars and looked across toward Cabaret Island. Early that afternoon Matt had taken a party across. She scanned the beach and saw that the groups of people were preparing to come back from their outing. Carol wanted to keep busy and avoid thinking of her troubles, so she went down to the dock and took the launch to the island.

The river was bright in the late sun, and her eyes ached. Her head throbbed from her hangover. She wanted to quit early tonight, since she needed rest more than anything else.

The party on the island had done considerable drinking, and everyone was in high spirits on the ride back in the launch. Carol realized she would need to return to collect debris and possibly broken glass. She maintained her mission to preserve Cabaret Island.

One of the men came back and sat with Carol on the engine box. He tried to get familiar with her when his date was not looking.

"Look, buster," said Carol. "Go on up front with the others. I'm running a ferry service--and nothing else."

"I saw you around the dock when we started out. You've got what I'm after," he said drunkenly.

"What sort of girl do you think I am?" she asked narrowly.

He looked at her with lust in his eyes. "I've heard things about you. You're my kind of river rogue. Come on, how about it? One of the other guys will take my date home. She's a washout anyway."

"Get back upfront. I'm warning you," Carol picked up the wrench and rolled it between her hands.

He got the idea in an instant and glared at her indignantly. In a huff he staggered forward and rejoined his companions.

When the last passenger had been put ashore, Carol drew a deep sigh of relief. She helped Matt secure the launch for the night, and then trudged the stairs to the clubhouse.

Two pleasure boat owners came in off the river from a day's outing and paused in the clubhouse for refreshments. It was dark when Wally finally closed down the lunch counter. He left, and a peaceful solitude came to the Cabaret Boat dock.

Carol went outside and sat down on an upturned rowboat, as the stars began appearing in the heavens. She lit a cigarette and blew a cloud of smoke into the still air. She began to relax as she looked at the river, growing dark and enigmatic, as it rolled eternally on its way. She sat there, letting her mind roam at will.

Her thoughts were inconsequential, a crane winged its way home in the dusk, the soft rose-and-blue of the dying light in the western sky, the river that would hold her forever to its way of life. She had the conviction that she would never escape it now.

She tossed her cigarette away and got up. She dragged herself back into the clubhouse, turned off the lights and noticed the headlights of a car coming in from Riverview drive. She stood at the screen door, waiting to see who it was. The convertible rolled to a stop outside. A young woman got out. Under her arm was a newspaper. She glanced toward the clubhouse and saw Carol.

"You're the one I came to see," said Hadley grimly. She pushed her way into the clubhouse.

"What do you want?"

"I want to know the meaning of this and several other things." Hadley slapped the newspaper open to the story of last night. She waved it under Carol's nose. "I'm here to tell you that you'd better lay off my husband, or I'll put you out of business overnight."

Hadley's eyes were cold and accusing. She flaunted a chic yellow, shirtwaist dress with a dark-gray Channel jacket. Carol, in her faded shorts and tank top, felt inadequate as she faced her attacker. She never dreamed she would ever be accused of trying to take someone's husband. She eyed Hadley.

"Be careful what you say about me," Carol warned.

"You're the reason Monte wants a divorce," Hadley came back. Her words cracked like a whip-lash. "You're trying to get him involved with stuff like this."

Hadley flung the paper on a table. She glared at Carol, then sat down, crossed her long legs and lit a cigarette. Carol stood by the counter and watched her carefully.

"I had nothing to do with Monte's getting into that scrape last night. You can read what it says in the paper. I was on my way home with a friend and Monte happened to be awake when we reached the dock. It wasn't my fault."

"Who went in the river? Who pulled a cheap stunt just to get attention?" Hadley shot her a contemptuous look.

"You're crazy. I fell in."

Hadley studied her. "I came here to tell you to leave my husband alone. Do you understand?"

"I'm not bothering him."

Hadley scoffed. "Not much, you aren't. I know all about you. You've done everything you can to get him to leave me."

"You haven't been living together for the past six months. Monte told me about you."

Here Hadley lowered her voice and a thin smile crossed her mouth. "You're on pretty shaky ground, I happen to know you owe people lots of money. How'd you like to wake up one morning and find this place didn't belong to you any longer?"

Carol stared back, "You can't do anything to me."

You think not? I happen to know Frank Weaver, and I know Conrad Ebbs, one of the owners of the estate. They hold a lot of mortgages around this town and one of them happens to be on your place."

Just you dare try interfering with my business. Said Carol between her teeth.

"The same goes for you and my marriage. Get that through your thick skull. I'm not going to be laughed at in St Louis by giving Monte a divorce so he can go and marry you. People will think he left me because he fell for a common river girl."

Carol recognized this woman now for what she was, a deadly enemy. She would stop at nothing. Until this moment Carol had given little thought to her, other than the fact that Hadley had Monte over a barrel. That was not enough for Hadley. She was trying to get Carol over the same barrel, and for all Carol knew she might succeed.

"I'm not after your husband," Carol said quietly.

"Who're you trying to kid?" Hadley asked scornfully. "I wasn't born yesterday, and neither were you. Don't tell me you haven't given Monte a good time. You're coaxing him right out of his head."

"Don't you dare talk to me that way. Get out of here." Carol's temper exploded.

"How often have you two spent the night together—talking about boats?" Hadley smiled.

"Did you hear me? Get out."

Carol's rage mounted. No one could talk to her like that and get by with it. The sight of Hadley calmly sitting there, made Carol's blood boil.

"You can't throw me out of a place that you can't call your own. Now about Monte—" Hadley said.

"What about him?" Carol raged. Her fury was giving her new life.

"Are you going to let him go or do I have to get my friends to move in on you?"

"Do whatever you damn please, but get out." Carol screamed.

Hadley stood up. She was taller than Carol by several inches. She smiled haughtily and looked on Carol as someone from the other side of the tracks; someone to be dealt with then dismissed.

"Very well, you asked for it. I'm not one to hold back," Hadley said and turned to go.

Carol's temper got the best of her. Hadley had so enraged her that she hardly knew what she was doing. Carol pushed the smartly dressed woman toward the door. Hadley flung her arm back in an effort to shove Carol away and dignify her exit, but in doing so her hand struck Carol's cheek. Carol charged in a blind fury.

For a shocked instant, Hadley retreated with no other thought than getting out. Then she too was caught up into a rage. She was not going to be bullied around by a river tramp. She clawed at Carol.

Carol's initial charge carried enough force to put Hadley off balance. Both women went down. Carol landed on top, but she did not stay there long. Hadley was like a trapped tigress. She fought with such fury that Carol was thrown off her and across the floor. Before she could get up, Hadley rushed at her and began kicking.

In desperation Carol grabbed Hadley's knees. Carol was dazed as she felt fists whacking down on her head. She rolled away to avoid being kicked again.

Hadley followed, sensing victory. "Maybe this will teach you a lesson, damn you," she swore.

Carol felt blow after blow falling upon her. Blindly she clutched out. Her hand caught the woman's jacket and there was a ripping sound. For an instant, Hadley's arms were pinned to her side by the jacket. Carol staggered to her feet, but Hadley jerked out of the jacket. She grabbed Carol and threw her down. Carol had only enough time to get up on one elbow before Hadley leaped upon her. She sank under the opponent's crushing weight.

Carol blanked out for a second. When she regained her senses, Hadley had her pinned down to the floor. She groaned with a supreme effort to get free but Hadley held her powerless. Carol's strength vanished. Her endurance had been tested to the limit last night, almost drowning in the current; she could take no more. She sobbed with despair and humiliation.

"For this you're going to lose everything," Hadley advised, using Carol's chest as a seat. "Monte and your business and preservation of Cabaret Island, as well."

Carol groaned and tried to move. The woman's taunting laughter gave Carol a sudden hysterical strength. She threw her off and rolled over to her hands and knees. She was so weak she could not arise. Hadley hurled herself at her again, and Carol sank to her stomach. She lay exhausted with Hadley kneeling on her back.

"Had enough?" cried Hadley, punishing her without mercy.

Carol clenched her teeth in agony. Just as she thought she could stand no more, the screen door opened and Monte came in. His eyes widened. He ran to the women and pulled them apart. As the pressure was lifted from her, Carol gasped for breath.

"What the hell's going on here?" he demanded.

"Do you think I'm going to let a river tramp interfere with my plans? She's not going to get away with it," Hadley screamed.

"Get away with what?" he asked grimly.

"As if you don't know." Hadley came back.

Carols mind came back to reality. She lost control and began to weep. An excruciating pain made her hand and shoulders throb where Hadley had hit her. She rose up from the floor to a kneeling position, hardly knowing what she was doing. Monte helped her to her feet. She swayed unsteady as she looked at him through the tears that filled her eyes.

"What's your side of the story, Carol?" Monte asked.

It was a moment before she could speak. "She insulted me. I told her to get out."

"Nothing could insult you." Hadley flung the words back at her.

"I don't know why you came here in the first place, Hadley" said Monte, regarding his wife peculiarly.

"I saw what was in the paper. That little witch is trying to hook you. Are you too dumb to figure that out?"

"That's the first time I knew you cared a damn what happened to me," he commented.

Hadley glared at him. "Don't think I've changed my mind any about that, but when a scheming river girl is out after your money, that's where I come in. Don't forget there's a heck of a lot that remains to be settled between you and me."

Though Carol's senses were dulled, Hadley's word stung. It was the first time the question of money had entered into it.

"You're a liar." Carol accused. "Money had nothing to do with it."

"I know what sort of a fix you're in here. You'd do anything to latch onto some cash, you—"

Carol swung with all the strength she had left. It was not much. Her fist landed on Hadley's jaw sending the startled woman back a pace. Monte stepped in and held the women apart. Hadley soothed her jaw gently, and Carol felt that she had avenged herself, in part, for her earlier defeat.

"I'm going. Don't worry," said Monte's wife. "And I'm going to see to it that there are some changes made quickly around this shanty." She wheeled about, flung open the door and slammed it sharply behind her.

Monte looked at Carol. "What's this talk about money?" he asked.

"I don't know. I don't know anything," without another word Carol turned and stumbled to her room. She was numb. Her arms and legs ached cruelly as she got undressed. She dragged herself on to the bed. All she wanted was oblivion.

Before she dropped off to sleep one solid thought came to her. If Hadley went to Frank Weaver and conspired against her, Carol's goose would be cooked. She could not hold out forever against the combined forces of a man who had her strapped financially and a wife who stood in the way of her love.

11   Frank is Obsessed

Bill Raft phoned in the bad news two days later. It was going to cost twelve hundred dollars to have his boat repaired. Carol received the call at the clubhouse and told Monte when he came up for breakfast.

"What are we going to do?" she asked.

"Leave that to me. I'm going to have a talk with Joe Mosley. It's only fair that he and I split the expense."

"You can't talk to Joe. You'll get into another fight with him."

"No. I'm going to see him right away—this morning. That's one piece of business that can be finished quickly."

She tried to talk him out of it. But by that time he finished breakfast and was ready to leave for town. Carol's pleading with him did no good; Monte's mind was made up. He felt that the issue was clear cut. He wanted to settle it himself with Joe.

Butterflies flitted inside her stomach as Monte drove off. She wondered if he would come back whole if, indeed, he was able to get back at all. He had held his own with Joe the other time they tangled but that did not mean he could do it again. Joe was a powerful, young river man. His love for Carol was crude and turbulent like the Mississippi itself. He recognized no rules of sportsmanship in a fight, especially a grudge fight.

She should not have let Monte go. As the morning wore on, Carol blamed herself more and more for not finding some way of keeping him back. Matt reported that some of the planks on the dock across on the Cabaret Island where the launch unloaded passengers needed attention, and debris remained from several days ago, but Carol was too nervous to look into it. She might have worked herself into an even higher pitch had not the appearance of Frank Weaver given her something else to worry about.

"What's going on around here?" he asked, sitting down at her desk. "Conrad Ebbs, one of the big wheels of the estate, asked me to look into things. He had been talking to-"

"So Hadley didn't lose any time, did she?" Carol injected.

"That's right. I was surprised to find out she even knew about this place. In fact, I was surprised to find out a lot of things I didn't know before." Frank smiled.

"What are you going to do?"

"I don't know. I told Ebbs not to worry, that I was looking after the best interests of the estate."

"That's a laugh."

He studied her with amusement. "Which side are you on, Carol? I was covering up for you when I told him that."

"And for yourself?" she added sardonically.

"Regardless," he said, "I think you'd better reduce your loan by another thousand dollars. That'll put us on a safe side for a while longer."

"I've got as much chance of paying you a thousand dollars right now as I have of buying the Chain of Rocks Bridge."

"Then you're in real trouble, Carol, and there's only one way out."

Their eyes met. She looked at him, hating the glint she saw in his expression. It made her feel cheap and tawdry, in the same class with other low-lives who sold out. What burned her up was that Frank Weaver believed he could buy her.

"You dirty, filthy rat," she said with all the venom she could get into her words.

His face darkened. "Talk that way if you want. If it wasn't for me, you'd be out of here right now. I've been protecting you."

"Why?"

"You know why." His voice was almost a whisper. "I'm crazy for you Carol. I've got to have you. And I will. I'm going to make love to you if it's the last thing I do." His words had a tinge of insane lust before he finished.

Frank picked cat hairs from his shirt.

Mastering this golden girl - spawned, nursed and reared by the river - had become an obsession with Frank Weaver. All of his uneventful life he had dreamed of taking a first choice because in reality nothing but leftovers were available to him. Girls, the desirable ones, never gave him a chance. He had always looked on while other more attractive men walked off with the prizes. With Carol he found himself in a position of influence. He was determined to use it to his advantage. Just as insidious as the river chewing at a sand bank, Frank sought to savor her delicious charms.

"You're crazy," she said.

"If I am, it's because I'm crazy about you. You'd better begin figuring how you're going to get another thousand dollars, or settle things another way. I can't keep the trustees quiet unless it's worth my while. I know you've fallen for Monte, and it's got me worried. I've got to use any advantage."

Out of curiosity she asked, "What guarantee would I have that you could keep the trustees off me, even if I agreed?"

"Just leave that to me. I look after the books for the estate."

Carol shook her head in bewilderment. She could not understand how a man could so completely lose his head. He was a simpleton, a nitwit, a fool. He was willing to sell himself in the purchase of her.

She felt sorry for the people who entrusted their business to Frank, but that was their worry, not hers.

"I don't know how I can raise any more money," she said.

"You don't have to do it today—and you wouldn't have to raise it at all, if you would do things my way, he told her. I can cover up quite a while for you."

"You know how I feel about that," she snapped.

"Then get another thousand dollars together in a week," said Frank sternly. He stood up and put on his straw hat; his chubby body had perspired through his seersucker suit. His red shiny face and thick, wet lips were no compromise to his gawking eyes at Carol.

Just before he left he said, "Carol, my patience with you is about at the end. I don't think even you can expect me to go on much longer, especially since there has been some heat put on your case."

I'll get even with Hadley somehow, Carol muttered to herself, not to Frank.

At noon Matt again reminded her of the plank repairs needed on the island dock, not mentioned the debris. He was afraid that someone might get hurt, unless it was fixed. Carol said she would have a look at it right after lunch. At one-thirty she went down to the dock and prepared to set out for the island in the launch. Just as she was ready to cast off, Monte came down the steps. Her heart leaped at the sight of him. He did not look as though he had been in a fight. She waited for him.

"Are you all right?" she asked, searching him with her eyes.

"Naturally. But that isn't the whole story. I didn't even see Joe Mosley. He's left town. They said he's gone down on the Tennessee River on a hitch that'll take several weeks."

Monte seemed agitated. That left him holding the bag with Bill Raft. After her first relief at finding that there had been no trouble between Joe and Monte, now she was faced with the guilt of being indebted to Monte for the cost of the boat damage.

Carol was still processing the latest developments as she headed the launch toward Cabaret Island. Gradually she began to tune in the calls of the mallards splashing down on the beach, the stalking cranes frozen in the shallows and the wild sweep of willow and river birch sparkling green in the afternoon sun. This peaceful oasis always eased her mind. She could not help smiling.

The repairs and collecting of debris grave her purpose and she resolved again to save this magical island at all cost.

The sun was an orange glow on the water as Carol finished her work and sank to the island dock. After the sticky heat of the day and her labors she welcomed the caress of the soft, southern breeze. In no time she was fast asleep and only dreamed the whisper, *Danger is here*.

12 Monte's Gift

The ease with which Monte disposed of Bill Raft stuck in Carol's mind for several days. It must be wonderful to have money. When things got too tough you just wrote a check. She thought of that again when Frank Weaver called to remind her that her week of grace was about up, and what was she going to do about it? She stood in the phone booth with the door open because the day was hot.

"I don't know what I can do about it," she told him.

"Yes, you do," Frank's voice came back soft, but insistent.

"How many times do I have to tell you, I won't do it that way?"

"I'm warning you, Carol. You'd better have the money for me tomorrow. If you don't, I'm going to foreclose. There's no other choice open to me." He lowered his voice even more, " – it's that or else."

Her forehead was damp as she held the receiver. She had been taxing her brains, trying to think of ways to get another thousand dollars for him. She was at the end of her rope.

Her restraint disappeared. She shouted at him over the phone. "Okay, if that's the way you feel about it, go ahead. Take the place over I'll get out. It'll be a relief not to have you yapping at me constantly."

"I'll be out to see you tomorrow," Frank put in hastily.

She hung up. She was so chocked with anger and frustration that she could not have seen anything more if she had wanted to. Tears of bitterness and defeat blurred her eyes as she stepped out of the booth. Hadley was having her fun. She had struck Carol where it hurt the most.

Carol was not aware of Monte, who had stopped in the clubhouse. He had just returned from a visit with his lawyer in town.

"What on earth is going on?" he asked, gazing at her in bewilderment.

"It's that wife of yours. She's put the blood hounds on me good. I'm about to lose my business."

Carol walked to the counter and sat down. Wally had gone to Baden for some supplies, and she and Monte were alone in the clubhouse. Monte followed her and sat on a stool at her side. He had not known about this before and wanted the details.

Carol told him everything, omitting only the alternative Frank Weaver had suggested countless times. She saw no point in telling Monte about that. When she finished he sat pondering.

"I wish I had known about this before," he said finally.

"It wouldn't have done any good." Carol smiled.

"It all ties in. I've known for some time that Hadley is out to wreck me. When she tries to throw the hooks into you as well, that's going too far."

"But I owe the money. I don't deny that. All she's doing is hastening the day when my creditors will move in on me."

"I'm not too sure about that," said Monte. "I'd rather help you out with my money than see others get it."

Carol spun around to face him. "No. I'm not borrowing any more money from anybody. I owe too much already."

"You wouldn't be borrowing it. In a way, it would be just keeping it in the family. If Hadley ever lets me go—"

"But what if she doesn't."

"We'll worry about that later. What did you say you have to pay by tomorrow? A thousand dollars?"

Carol nodded gloomily.

"Come on down to the boat with me," said Monte.

"What for?"

"You'll see." He grinned and took her arm. Carol went with him. They descended the steps to the dock and walked to the slip where Monte's cruiser was tied up. He told her to hop aboard and have a seat.

She heard him mixing some cocktails in the galley. Then he went on into his living quarters for a moment. When he appeared again, he had a small tray with two cocktail glasses on it. Under one of the glasses was a check.

"Take the check, too," he said, when she lifted one of the drinks.

Carol picked it up. She stared at it in wonder. It was hard for her to believe—a check for one thousand dollars. Her eyes filled with tears as she looked up at him. "You shouldn't do this, Monte. It just isn't right." A deep gratitude undermined her protest.

"I'd rather help you than anybody else in the world. Now, you go ahead and pay the fellow who's been racking you, and quit worrying."

"You'll never know how much this means to me, Monte."

Her adoring eyes gazed at him. This thousand dollars probably meant no more to him than ten would to her. That was the way it was when you were rich. But it was not the money that counted just now with Carol. It was the fact that he wanted to help her. That made her feel good all over. A radiant smile crossed her face. She lifted her glass.

"Thank you, Monte. Thank you, so very much."

Later, they were joined by Chuck Sherman and his wife, Louise. The Shermans owned a cruiser and occasionally put in at the Cabaret Dock. They traveled up and down the river a good deal. In no time at all, Monte and the other couple were fast friends. They too were well off and Monte shared stories with them.

What had started as a pleasant visit ended at midnight with the four of them taking off in Monte's boat for the island and a swim by moonlight. Carol's heart was bursting with love for Monte when finally she left his boat just before dawn.

She awoke the next morning in her own bed, with a new lease on life. She got more work done around the dock that morning than she had in a week. She kept an eye out for Frank, who had said he would be out that day to get his money or find out what other arrangements she had decided to make. She looked forward to his visit and the vengeful satisfaction she would get at handing him the check. He came in shortly after lunch. Carol decided to have a little fun with him.

"Come on back to the desk, Frank," she said.

She sat down and lit a cigarette. He held out his lighter for her. After she had taken a puff she leaned back and gave him a long, studious look. "I can't pay you with cash," she told him.

"I gathered that from what you said on the telephone. That's too bad, Carol. I hate to see you lose your business. I know it means a lot to you, since it belonged to your father. I'd do anything to help you keep it?"

"Anything?"

"Certainly I'm even willing to take a risk, as I have told you," he said softly.

"But only if I come across."

"Don't you think I'm entitled to something?" he smiled.

"I've been thinking about that." She studied her cigarette. Yes, you are entitled to something.

His eyes widened. He had not been prepared for such a ready agreement. It was far more than he had hoped for. There was dubiousness in his words. "Don't tell me you've come around to seeing things my way."

"Could be."

Frank sat forward on the edge of his chair. His eyes danced with excitement. "You really mean you'll – well-"

"That depends. There's some risk involved for me, too. You know. I wouldn't ever want people to know what I'd done to hang on here."

"Oh, believe me, Carol, no one ever will. That will be our litte secret. Forever," he assured her.

"When would you want to start—collecting? And more importantly, where?"

"Tonight. Tomorrow night, he said, his anticipation growing by leaps and bounds. "I can wait a day or so. We'll suit your convenience. You'll never regret this, Carol. Never, as long as you live."

She gave him a look of disillusionment. "Don't try to sell me the idea. You're forcing me to it, you know."

"It's just a little matter of expedience. That's all," he smiled at her intimately. "You'll learn to like me."

"Where do you propose to take me? You haven't said."

"We could go a tourist place. There are several around, I understand, where no questions are asked. Coral Courts on Route 66." Frank's heart was pounding so hard by this time, as visions of his reward swam through his head, that he had to stop and get his breath.

"Is that the best you can do?" she smiled thinly.

"But you said yourself that you didn't want to take any chances. What I've suggested would be the safest way."

" I don't like it, try again."

He looked at her in bewilderment. "I guess there are hotels where-"

"That's out, too."

It was all Carol could do to keep from laughing out loud at his confusion. He stared at her. If she disapproved of a tourist camp or a hotel, what did she have in mind? He racked his brain but could not find an answer.

"Where else did you think we could go," he asked blindly.

She tired of the game. Loathing came into her eyes and they flashed anger as she glared at him. "I know where you can go, and that's straight to hell."

"What?" His mouth dropped open.

"Why you sniveling, sneaking lug. Do you think I'd allow you to lay a finger on me? They shouldn't let skunks like you run around loose. If I was a man I'd kick you out of here and over the bank right into the river." She blazed with hatred.

It took him a minute to find words now, "You look here, Carol, I won't have."

"Suppose you do some looking." She retorted with sarcasm. With that she jerked open the center drawer of her desk and threw Monte' s check down in front of him.

Frank gaped at it a long time. His face darkened, he had been hoodwinked. Anger and frustration played havoc with him - this girl had heaped insult on injury. She had strung him along, knowing all the while that she was looking down his throat.

"Now get out of here." she ordered. "And if you come around one more time, I'm going to the trustees myself and complain about you. I'm going to tell them in person how you've been trying to use their influence for your own sneaking purpose. Now beat it, you bastard."

Frank Weaver shrank before her vehemence. He had never seen her so angry. For a second he held one arm up instinctively expecting her to start beating on him. When he realized what he was doing he tried hard to regain his composure. "You think you're pretty smart, don't you," he snarled.

"Any time I can't outsmart a fool like you, I'll give up."

Frank got to his feet; his face was as red as a beet. His eyes shifted and his fat body trembled with resentment. He grabbed up Monte's check and stuck in his pocket, glaring at her. She need not think he was through. Not by a long shot. He would find a way. He would think of something, he would humble this girl if it was the last thing he did. Without a word he turned and left the clubhouse.

Carol sat at the desk, calming herself. The fruits of her revenge went beyond Frank Weaver. She despised him, but it was Hadley who was on her mind now. Hadley's attempt to do her in through Conrad Ebbs was contemptible. If possible, they would sell out Cabaret Island and Cabaret Boat Dock to the local investors who wanted to make an amusement park. Hadley's efforts had put Frank in a position to pressure her so soon after her last payment. Carol had given the girl her answer, with her own husband's money.

"Cap'n," said Matt, breaking into her thoughts, "the bilge pump on the launch ain't working right."

"It isn't?" she looked up at Mat and smiled. "Well, we'll have to do something about that. Let's go have a look at it," her voice rang with confidence.

Matt followed her out, shaking his head. Sometimes she sounded just like her father used to, when Matt was a roustabout on a boat piloted by Sam Burke. Matt smiled with affection at the girl who descended the steps to the dock in front of him. Sam would be proud of her, he thought, but sooner or later Matt would need to reveal to Carol that she was a descendent of the Iroquois nation and what happened to her mother – last seen in 1936.

"I thought I told you to stay away from here," Carol exclaimed.

It was mid-morning, one week later. The sun had risen in a cloudless sky, and the thermometer had already pushed into the nineties. Carol had just returned from the boats as a car stopped in front of the clubhouse. Frank Weaver got out and stood before her.

"That's right, you did," he sneered.

She knew at once that he had something up his sleeve. Frank had figured out some other way to bedevil her, but she no longer feared him. Her threat to go directly to the trustees had not been an idle one. She was not going to take any more guff from Frank Weaver.

"What have you dreamed up this time?" she demanded. "Speak up and be quick about it. I don't want the place dirtied up with you around."

"I didn't come to see you."

"Well, if you think you're going to bother my customers, you've got another thing coming. What do you want?"

"I want to see the author of this check."

Carol looked at the thousand-dollar check Monte had written as Frank held it in front of her. He had taken her by surprise. She looked up at him. "Well?"

"It bounced all the way back from Cincinnati."

"I don't believe that," she flared.

Frank gave an insolent chuckle. "Maybe you'll believe what the bank in Cincinnati says."

He pointed out the wording, rubber-stamped on the check. INSUFFICIENT FUNDS. Carol stared at it, unwilling to believe what she saw. *If this was another one of his tricks.*

"There's some mistake," she asserted. "Monte has plenty of money."

"He'd better have a thousand dollars to cover this check. Where is he? I've to find out what he's going to do about it."

"I'll go get him, she said. You wait here."

Carol went down to the dock. She knew there was some error about the check. Monte could clear it up in no time. She walked along the dock to his cruiser.

"Monte?" she called.

"What-o?" his voice came from deep within the boat.

She stepped across and peered into the deck house. Monte came up from the engine compartment where he had been resetting the water pump. He wiped his hands on a rag and smiled at her.

"The fellow I gave your check to is up at the clubhouse, Monte. There's been some mistake," she said.

"That so? What sort of mistake?"

"It failed to clear the bank where it was drawn."

The smile faded from his face. His brows knitted. "I can't understand that. Wait'll I wash my hands. I'll go up and see what it's all about."

Five minutes later Carol and Monte mounted the steps. Frank idled about the clubhouse grounds, looking around as if he had a proprietary interest in the place. Frank came over when they appeared.

"I guess Carol told you what I'm here for," Frank said

"Yes. Let me see the check."

Frank held it, but was not about to let it go. Monte read the stamped inscription and frowned.

"Of course, there's been a mistake."

"Probably so," Frank conceded. "Suppose you just give me the cash, and I'll give you back the check. That'll take care of it."

"I don't carry a thousand dollars in my pocket," Monte said, looking at him as if he was crazy. "I'll have to call my bank. They'll verify my account and you can send the check through again, or I'll write you a new one."

With that he went into the clubhouse and disappeared into the telephone booth. Frank followed him inside and walked to the counter where he ordered a bottle of soda. He offered Carol one, but she refused. She sat on a stool, aloof and impatient. Frank would be put back in his place as soon as Monte finished talking to his bank.

"It's taking a long time for him to find out if he's overdrawn," Frank commented as he glanced at his wrist-watch.

"Don't forget he had to make a long-distance call to Cincinnati."

Frank only smiled. He finished his bottle of soda while Monte had been in the phone booth for more than ten minutes. Even Carol was beginning to wonder at the delay but she did not let on in front of Frank. She would not give him the satisfaction.

The door of the booth opened and Monte came out. There was a dazed look on his face. He was wringing wet with sweat. He mopped his brow with a handkerchief and tugged at his collar. "Wow. It's hot in there," he said.

"What did you find out?" Frank asked.

Monte glanced at him. "There's been a mistake."

"Then maybe you'd better write me a new check or give me the money. Either way-"

"No, it's a different kind of mistake," Monte interrupted.

"Haven't you got the money?"

"I don't know. You'll have to wait."

"Now look here, Monte. You've written a bum check and- "

"Hell, it's not my fault," Monte snapped. "Do you think I did it on purpose?"

"I didn't say that, but the fact remains. He held the check in his hand. You'd better pick this up with cash."

Carol saw by Monte's expression that something had gone wrong. Concern showed in her eyes. He had written the check to help her; she did not want to cause him any trouble on her account

"I've got to see my lawyer before I can tell you anything. I'm going into town right now," Monte said quickly. With that he left the clubhouse.

Carol ran out after him. "Monte, what is it?"

"I don't know, sweet. I'll find out what I can from my lawyer and let you know when I get back."

He was deeply agitated and anxious to be off. A strange feeling came over her. She had never seen Monte so worried about anything. He hurried to his car and drove off. She went back into the clubhouse, plunged in thought.

"What do you think now, was I right or not?" Frank asked sarcastically.

"He'll straighten it out," she replied.

"I'll say he will. I won't hesitate one second to turn this phony check over to the city circuit attorney for action."

Carol's eyes widened. Sudden fear was in her glance. "No. You can't do that."

She bit her lip. Frank's eyes gleamed at her. He had caught the terror in her voice. Suddenly, he knew there was something more to this than met the eye.

"I know he'll straighten it out," she added lamely.

"When? That's the point."

A fear gnawed at her insides. She could not let Monte suffer prosecution because he had been trying to help her out. He had not deliberately written a bad check.

"You wouldn't like to see him go to jail, eh?" Frank observed.

"Of course, I wouldn't. Not because of an honest mistake."

She tried to cover her apprehension. She did not dare let Frank know how important this was to her, but he was not to be sidetracked. He had discovered a weakness.

"That guy means an awful lot to you, doesn't he?" It wasn't a question. Frank was making a statement.

"You've got to give him time. Even the authorities would do that."

"Of course, they would. They'd tell him to pay up or face arrest. And I'm telling you right now that he'll pick up this check first thing in the morning, or I'm going to the Circuit Attorney's office. Now, what have you got to say about that?" Frank smirked.

"He will. I'm not in the least worried about that."

"There is only one thing that can hold me off, Carol." he went on. "Will you guarantee payment of this, one way or another?" He waved the check to taunt her.

Carol smoldered as she looked at him. Her lips were compressed into a thin, straight line. She was not afraid of his threats. She knew Monte could be counted on and replied between her teeth, "Yes."

"Then I'll see you bright and early in the morning."

With that Frank turned and drove away. Carol lit a cigarette, barely able to hold her nerves steady. Doubts poured into her mind as she recalled the look on Monte's face just before he left. Something had happened, no question about that. She was distressed to think that it had been about a check he had written for the sole purpose of helping her out of a predicament.

She could not bear the thought of his being arrested on her account. She would have to prevent Frank from going to the circuit attorney at any cost. He did not know it for sure, but he had a much more effective weapon in that check than he had ever had in the threats to put her out of business.

Carol was unable to keep her mind on her work. No matter how quickly Monte was able to contact his lawyer, it would still take him a couple of hours to get into town and back.

After lunch she looked around every time a car passed on Riverview Drive, wondering if it would turn in, or if it was Monte. Her anxiety mounted as the afternoon wore on.

He came back at five o'clock. She was down on the dock, trying to fix a leaking pontoon with Matt's help when Monte came down the steps. She quit work immediately and hurried to him. She searched his eyes. "What is it, Monte?" she asked anxiously.

"What isn't it?" he said flatly. "Oh brother."

"You mean the check is really no good?" her heart sank.

"Come aboard the boat. I really need a drink."

Monte made a couple of highballs and sat down with her in the cockpit. He drank half of his in one gulp. Then he wagged his head in despair.

"Hadley has hit me with everything in the law books," he began slowly. "There is a joint account we had in the Cincinnati bank I hadn't bothered to do anything about in all this time. That was my first mistake. Just a few days ago, she cleaned that out, but good."

At those words, Carol drank half of her highball too. Monte went on. "We had some other property in joint ownership. She's got that tied up, too, pending a settlement with her by way of a divorce, or separate maintenance, or whatever finally happens."

Carol's mouth went dry despite her drink. "But how could she do that?"

"As it turns out, the lawyer I'd hired in town had been a stool pigeon all this time. Hadley's lawyer made a monkey out of him, and me. They want local amusement park investors to get control of Cabaret Island and Boat Dock. Don't ask me how she did it, but they did. And it was all quite legal, apparently."

Carol swallowed hard. "Does that mean you can't cover the check you wrote?"

"Yes, and I wish that was all I had to worry about," he laughed mirthlessly.

"What- what are you going to do, Monte?"

"Right now, I feel like getting drunk."

"But, I mean about-" she stopped. The thousand-dollar check was no longer his worry. It was hers. He had just stated that the check was only a small part of his misfortune. Hadley had taken him to the cleaners in more ways than the joint bank account.

"Let me get you a refill," said Monte.

Carol looked at her glass in astonishment. She had been so distracted by a feeling of impending doom, that she had not been aware of emptying it. She handed it to him.

Carol too, felt like getting drunk.

13   Disappearing Act

A merciless sun poured heat onto the earth and the river as Carol awoke the following morning. She groaned as the light stabbed her eyes. Her head throbbed with every beat of her pulse, and her mouth tasted parched, like a cast-off sponge. She made her way to the bathroom and gulped down three large glassfuls of water. It abated the turbulence that raged in her but only for a few minutes.

She sat on the edge of the bed, trying to bring herself under control. Fleeting thoughts of last night came to her mind. It had turned into a drinking spree for both Monte and her. She could not recollect the approximate time the gloom had turned into intoxication, but it had and abruptly, it had been as if both were intent upon drowning their problems.

She remembered that they had decided with what had seemed to be great logic at the time, to go to the harbor in Monte's cruiser and have dinner at the Skipper's Inn. They had spent a roaring evening there and moved on to catch the last act aboard Captain Bliss's showboat, an ancient theatrical enterprise that had been operating at the St Louis Levee for a year.

They had hissed the villain and encouraged the heroine and had been the special guest of Captain Bliss on top of the deck after the show for mint juleps. Carol had known the old showboat captain for years.

Monte said, "I never saw anything like it. I'm telling you, it's the greatest entertainment discovery since the Greek tragedies." They had gone back up the river to the Cabaret dock when Monte boasted through the liquor, "I'm going to buy a showboat for myself. What do you say? You're my heroine and I'll protect you from the villain every night."

The night had not ended with that. She could not remember the last rapturous throbs in Monte's arms. With a zing from her heart to her groin and back, deep orgasms seemed to go on and on forever. But now an aching reality reminded her that it had ended. A long day of recovery lay ahead.

She drank a cup of coffee that Wally poured for her at the lunch counter. It was ten-thirty. Carol was scolding herself for sleeping so late when Frank Weaver arrived. The sight of him changed her disposition from bad to worse.

"Where's the boy friend? Has he got my money?" Frank asked.

"He hasn't had time. I don't think he's even awake yet." She looked at him sullenly over the rim of her coffee cup.

"Where is he? On his boat?"

"How should I know?"

Frank gave her an exasperated look. She saw him disappear outside and down the steps toward the dock. Carol concentrated on the black coffee stimulating life back into her body. She had a lot of work to do today. Frank was back just as she finished the cup.

"He's not there," he said.

"Maybe he went into town to get you straighten out. That would make sense, wouldn't it?" she gritted her teeth.

"You're sure evil as hell this morning," Frank said. "Can't you get the barbed wire out of your voice for a minute so we can talk things over?"

"Look. Just run along," she said. "I'm not in any mood to take your nagging." Carol started back to her desk.

"It isn't very likely that he went to town in his boat, is it?"

Carol stopped. She turned around and started at Frank angrily. "Of course not. Now don't bother me anymore."

"Monte's boat is gone, too."

"You're nuts."

"Well, have a look for yourself, then."

At first she felt the urge to ignore him but there was no point in Frank's saying Monte's cruiser was gone if it was still there. She began to wonder about it herself.

She walked out of the clubhouse and looked down at the dock. She stared incredulously at the slip where Monte's boat had been docked. It was empty.

"Is it there? Am I blind?" asked Frank, coming up behind her.

Carol did not hear him. Monte's disappearance, along with his boat, came as a shock. She scanned the river. The cruiser was nowhere is sight. Matt was wiping the windows of the launch with a chamois. She cupped her mouth with her hands, and yelled down to him. "Hey, Matt do you know where Mr. Abbot went?"

Matt looked around and yelled back "He took off early this morning, Cap'n. Didn't say were he was going or whether or not he'd be back."

Carol did not know what to think. She stood there dumbfounded trying to find a reason for Monte's disappearance. A growing foreboding spread through her nerves, stimulating her more than the coffee, but not a pleasant way.

"Looks like he's slipped away," Frank observed.

"He has not."

"What makes you so sure? He knew I'd be here for my money this morning."

"Monte isn't one to run out on a thing like that," said Carol.

"Regardless of what you say, he's gone. Now how about this here bounced check?"

"Oh, be quiet. He'll be back. You'll get your filthy money," she stormed back around, partly because of Frank and partly because Monte had gone off without telling her where he was headed and why.

She headed back to the clubhouse. Just as she reached the door a convertible arrived. Hadley slid out from behind the wheel, and a man wearing tortoise-rimmed glasses and carrying a briefcase got out from the other side. Frank shook hands with Hadley and was introduced to Thomas Dillon, whom Hadley identified as her attorney.

"Where's Monte? We're looking for him," said Hadley.

"I'm looking for him too," Frank smiled. "He's gone."

Hadley directed daggers at Carol, "I guess you know where he is. Well?"

"I don't know," Carol answered, locking eyes with the woman. Dillon stepped forward. A calm head was needed at this moment and he would be the man for the job. He knew how Hadley felt about Miss Carol Burke. She had told him in no uncertain terms. Now, glimpsing the girl for the first time, he conceded that Hadley had good reason for feeling as she did. Carol was a knockout.

"Suppose we go inside and talk it over," Dillon said aloud. "I'm sure Miss Burke will cooperate with us in locating him." He gazed at Carol warmly. "It's important, Miss Burke, or we wouldn't be bothering you."

"I told you I don't know where he is," said Carol.

"But surely he said something that might give us a clue."

"If he did, I sure wouldn't tell you." Carol glared at Hadley.

"Do you see what I mean about her?" Hadley exploded.

"I'm sure we can work this out," Dillon pushed out both arms like a wrestling referee.

Carol went into the clubhouse. As far as she was concerned, that ended it. She reached her desk and was startled to see Dillon and Hadley come in after her. Behind them Frank weaseled in to listen in if there was a chance of locating Monte Abbott.

"I told you, I don't know anything about it," Carol announced when they approached her desk. "I've got work to do. I can't be bothered with your problems."

"Tell me, Miss Burke," said Dillon in a brisk, business-like voice, "does Abbott owe you any money? If he does, it might be in your interest to help us find him. He was a customer of yours here, I understand."

"The money customers spend at the Cabaret Dock is none of your business," she blurted out to Dillon. It had never occurred to Carol to think of what Monte owed her. *His credit was good. Wasn't it?* Carol stood up and felt her stomach clench as she took in small breaths.

"I'm only saying that for your benefit. Abbott owes others. From the look of things, he's in bad financial trouble. And things are just getting worse."

Carol was about to pin the blame on Hadley. From what Monte had said, his wife was responsible. But she held her tongue. That was something she had no right to talk about.

Dillon decided he had scored a point when she did not reply. He smiled coaxingly. "Now will you tell us what you know as to his whereabouts?"

"Yes, I'll tell you. I know nothing." She eyed the three of them.

"Let's put it this way, Miss Burke," said Dillon, trying a different approach. "Do you know the whereabouts of his cruiser?"

"What are you trying to do, get that away from him too?" asked Carol as it occurred to her that it was the boat and not Monte that they wanted.

Hadley put her nose into the air. She looked at Carol as if she was dirt. Then she whirled around and walked out. Frank sauntered after her, but Dillon remained for a last word.

"Are you sure you don't know," he watched her closely.

"You heard me. He'd be more likely to tell his wife where he was going, wouldn't he?"

"Let's be honest, Miss Burke. You and Monte – er, Mr. Abbott- have been a lot closer lately than he and his wife."

"Who told you that?"

"Hadley – I mean Mrs. Abbott."

"That bitch is apt to say anything," Carol commented. "I know what kind she is. She's taking him through the ringer. Now please leave. You've wasted enough of my time. I don't know where Monte is, and if I did I wouldn't tell you. Is that clear enough for you?"

Dillon lost no time in getting out, after leaving his business card on her desk. Carol sank to her chair. She was still in a daze over Monte's disappearance. The visit of Hadley and her lawyer aroused a growing doubt in her mind. She opened the desk's drawer and took out a ledger book. Monte's account showed that he had run up close to a hundred dollars in charges since he had been at the Cabaret Dock.

She still could not believe that he had run out on her, or that he was a deadbeat. Yet, on the evidence he had left, he owed her a sizeable amount of money. That did not look good. That lawyer had said he owed money to others as well. She picked up the lawyer's business card and fought against the doubt that he had awakened within her.

She heard a car start outside and take off. A moment later, Frank Weaver came back inside. He sauntered to the desk to sit down.

"Looks as though we're not the only ones Abbott has clipped," he said. "Hadley and Dillon just told me he's got a lot of outstanding bills in Cincinnati."

"You can believe them if you want to."

"I sure don't want to, but it'll take a thousand dollars in cash to convince me otherwise- or a little convincing from you. You're the one, of course who is responsible for the payment. All I've got on Abbott now is a bad check." Carol's emotions had been assailed so thoroughly in the past half hour that she was no longer capable of standing up to anyone. She merely eased back in her chair, staring ahead, wondering what would happen next.

"Guess I'll run into town and turn this over to the authorities," Frank remarked as he took the check from his pocket and looked at it.

Carol bit her lip. In one respect, she was not responsible. Monte had volunteered to give her the money. She could wash her hands of it, but her heart cried out against such disloyalty. He had not known the check would bounce when he wrote it. He had stood by her, though later events had altered his position.

"Is that what you want me to do?"

"Of course not, but I can't stop you."

"Yes, you can."

"You're worse than a heel, using that as a threat," she said bitterly.

"You've called me worse names than that, Carol. I've gotten used to them by now and it's almost a turn-on for me. They'll catch Abbott sooner or later and put him in jail for this. Maybe he's got it coming."

Carol looked away frantically and clenched her teeth. She could not bear the thought of Monte ending up in the pokey on her account, and in this case it would be for no other reason. She could save him that ordeal. It was more than his wife would do for him.

"Writing a bad check of this size is a penitentiary offense – a felony. He could go up for as much as two years," Frank observed.

"It isn't," she cried.

"This is your last chance. If I leave here, I'm going directly to the civil courts building."

"Then go ahead. She covered her face with her hands and burst into tears."

Frank looked at her. He waited, but she did not look up. A sour expression crossed his moon-like face. His eyes grew hard with frustration and failure. Even with an ace like this rubber check he could not surmount this woman's resistance.

Grimly he got to his feet. "Okay, if that's the way you want it."

Carol's sobbed. Then she lowered her hands and despair was written all over her face. Her eyes were large and filled with hopelessness. Frank turned away from her desk. With each step he took toward the door, Carol's heart beat in wild rebellion. Like a caged animal with survival instincts of a tigress.

It hammered against her brain, driving reason to flight. A panic overtook her as Frank reached for the door's handle. She could not sacrifice Monte, no matter what. She loved him. In a burst of frenzy she knew that she would do anything for him, anything.

"Frank." she cried.

He looked over his shoulder, surprised. His hand was at the screen door. He hesitated.

"Wait a minute," Carol groaned.

He came back and stood over her at the desk. "What for?"

Carol bit her lip to keep it from trembling. "Don't turn in that check."

"But I've got no other choice."

"Yes, you have."

"You mean you'll---" a sly, lustful smile spread across his thick, wet lips. Carol lowered her head in defeat. What was the use trying to fight this any longer? Frank had her where he wanted her. Others would too, sooner or later. The creditors would start pouncing on her with regularity now. She was losing her business, just as surely as she had lost her heart to another financial failure like herself.

"Yes," she said weakly. "I'll do whatever you want."

14   Frank's Assault

Carol spent the next two days like a prisoner awaiting execution. It had been impossible for her to gratify Frank immediately. She was too exhausted for a date with him that very night, and the following night he had a business appointment which he could not cancel. Postponing his reward had been agreeable to him because it gave him many hours of delightful anticipation. His triumph was to come three nights later.

Carol performed her duties with apathy at the Cabaret Dock. She exhausted every possible means of getting out of the obligation to Frank, but there was simply no solution. Having been raised on the river, her word was as good as her bond, and she had given Frank her word. Even if she had renounced it, he had only to take the check to the circuit attorney.

Once or twice a ray of hope pierced her gloom. She glimpsed a white cruiser far down the river, headed her way. Monte's return was the only thing that would save her. She let herself believe that he would come back in time to prevent her from submitting to Frank. He had no way of knowing what she faced, of course, because she had never told him of the demands Frank Weaver had placed on her in lieu of cash payments. The cruiser turned out to belong to someone else. At closer range it did not even look like Monte's.

Carol faced her future with unflinching realism. She admitted to herself that she had failed. She was a woman trying to do a man's job. That might work in other places, but not on the river. A woman could not assert her independence. She couldn't even get a loan or bank account without her father's or husband's signature. The only thing left to her was to trade on her weakness, to bargain with the only advantage a woman had when dealing with men.

Once, she let herself get so depressed that she found that she was blaming Monte for her predicament. If he had managed his own affairs better, this would not be happening to her. She understood his weakness in not looking after his finances more carefully, but that did not make it any more palatable to her. He had let her down with a jolt. For a brief moment she even thought, to hell with him. Let him cool his heels in the clink for a while. It would teach him to be more careful.

Such thoughts occurred only fleetingly, however. Mostly, she did not think about her payment to Frank. It was an ordeal to be gotten over with. She approached it as an operation that could not be avoided.

Frank Weaver's attitude, meanwhile, was quite different. He was walking on clouds. When his day of victory dawned, he awoke early and was so excited that he could not go back to sleep. He phoned Carol that mid-morning and told her to be ready at seven o'clock that night. He had a surprise in store for her, and he asked her to dress for a special occasion.

Carol hung up after listening to him without even asking what the surprise was. The only thing that would have surprised her would be to get out of her commitment to him, and Frank would never let that happen.

At seven that evening she was dressed in a low-cut, navy-blue dress with a matching bolero jacket. Frank's eyes sparkled when he came for her. He sucked in his breath – *What a woman. And tonight you're all mine.*

"Ready?" he smiled.

"As ready as I'll ever be," she said indifferently.

"You're beautiful tonight, Carol. Simply magnificent and you'll be happy with what I've arranged."

Carol would not have been happy about anything, except being let off. They rode into town with Frank talking excitedly all the way and Carol sitting in the seat beside him staring glumly out the car window.

His surprise was dinner at the Club Plantation on Delmar, an air-conditioned night spot that boasted good food and a floor show with local entertainers. He had reserved a front-row table where he could bask in the light of Carol's radiance and be envied by everyone present. He thought, as he sat there, of the astonishment he would create if the other customers knew how completely he commanded this lovely woman.

Carol sensed his attitude, and her disgust mounted. Frank was making a production number out of his success. He was showing her off before leading her to slaughter. She had difficulty hiding her bitterness and decided to brace herself with cocktails for what was to come later. Frank downed three cocktails with manly gusto before dinner.

They ate, and Frank promptly ordered coffee and brandy with the dessert. "Nothing like a little brandy to settle a fine dinner like this," he said.

Carol glanced at him. His face was flushed and his grin was permanently affixed to his face. Her eyes narrowed but not enough for him to notice.

"I could take another brandy, Frank, if you don't mind," said Carol as a scheme began to take shape in her mind.

"My dear," he announced grandly. "You can have as many as you want," he gave her a huge wink. "This is our night. Good food, good liquor and good company."

Carol gave his hand a squeeze and Frank trembled with excitement. He ordered more drinks. When the floor show came on, he sat back and lit a cigar. A chorus line of six second-rate dancers and a master-of-ceremonies who told risqué jokes was the entertainment. The dancers were pretty and their scanty costumes were enticing.

Carol kept right on ordering drinks and Frank, entranced by the powerful aphrodisiac of the bare shoulders, bouncing breasts and flashing legs of the dancers went right along with her plan. By midnight he was dizzy with drink and desire.

"I've got just the place in mind for us now," he whispered. "Made inquiries about it - at the Coral Courts Motel out on highway Route 66."

"I was going to tell you earlier in the evening, but I've enjoyed myself so much that it slipped my mind."

"Look, Frank, why don't we go back to my place? There's no one around the clubhouse at this hour. We could have a nightcap before-" she broke off and smiled at him.

"Splendid," he agreed. He had fallen so thoroughly under her charm that he would have agreed to anything by then.

They left the Club Plantation. Carol noted with satisfaction that Frank had difficulty inserting the ignition key. The liquor he had drunk was beginning to work on him. Now, if she could get him to drink more at the clubhouse, there might yet be hope for her.

Frank was vaguely aware of his condition. He carefully drove all the way to the Dock. He did not want an accident, of all things, to ruin his night of nights.

Once at the Cabaret Dock, Carol led him through the darkened clubhouse and into her room. She pulled down the shade and got out a bottle of whiskey.

"Sit down, while I mix us a couple," she said.

"Come here a minute," Frank grinned.

Carol did as he asked. He took her in his arms, and for a moment he reveled in the triumph so long awaited. Nothing could stop him now. He lifted his lips to hers. Carol quickly turned her head so he would not see her revulsion.

"Fix the drinks," he ordered, drunk with exultation, to say nothing of alcohol.

Carol poured enough whiskey into his glass to finish him off for the rest of the night, if she could get him to drink it all. She poured just enough for herself to make things look authentic. They sat together on the sofa.

Frank held the drink in one hand, but the other could not resist the invitation of her. Carol's jaw was set. She dare not resist him now. The more encouragement she gave him, the more likely he was to drink the dangerous concoction. She smiled and touched her glass to his.

"Here's to us, Frank," she grinned. "May you always be able to hold off the trustees."

"I'll do it," he vowed, thrilled that she had finally entered into the conspiracy with him. He took a long guzzle from his glass. "Turn off the light and come here," he commanded.

"Where's the check? It's only fair that you give it to me in exchange."

Frank had difficulty focusing his eyes on her. "You'll get the check in due time. Come here now."

Carol regarded him. She was not going to let him keep the check He would hold it against her from now on. She would be saddled with him indefinitely if he did not turn it over to her now.

"But how do I know you'll give it to me?"

"Don't worry," he pulled her to him and grinned. "I'll give it to you tomorrow. Come on baby; let me squeeze your tits. Let's not argue at a time like this. We have much more interesting things to do". He finished his drink in one long gulp.

She did not for an instant believe him. Her mind raced. If she gave in to him without getting the check, it would all have to be done over again. Quite suddenly she knew that for sure.

"This isn't fair," she complained.

He could no longer be bothered with talk about the check. The time had come. He lunged for her. Carol's anger soared. She pulled away from him.

"How do I know you'll keep your word?" she demanded.

Frank did not answer her. He could not concentrate on anything but the need which gripped him. He grabbed her and pulled her to him again. In a moment of sudden fear, she jerked away from him.

Reason deserted him as her resistance fanned his desire. "Come here, you," he laughed hysterically.

Carol retreated in alarm. He had gotten out of hand. Instead of doing him in, as she had hoped, the liquor had made a beast of him.

"I'll go through with it," she cried. "But you've got to live up to your part of the bargain."

Frank did not even hear her. He could think of nothing but the ultimate reward. He came after her.

Carol fought to control the situation. She backed into a corner of the room, as far away from him as she could get. With faltering, stumbling steps he wove his way toward her.

"Come here, you bitch," he whispered, his eyes glinting.

Her reason gave way to panic. Instinctively she fought to protect herself. She slipped out of his reach and to the other side of the room - trying to escape to the porch outside. Frank staggered after her making a crazy giggle. Carol was cornered. Nothing mattered to her now but her escape.

He clutched her bare arm as she tried to run, and swung her to the floor. Carol fought like a wildcat. It was not his strength that she had to contend with, as much as his weight. For a terrible moment she felt as if she was being crushed. Blackness swam before her eyes, and she panted for breath.

"You can't get away from me now," he mumbled as he clung to her.

She thrashed about in agony, but he only snickered at her futile efforts. Her strength began to ebb. She groaned, and pleaded for his mercy. Frank was far beyond any human sympathy at this point. His long-denied passion was in full control. His mind was saddled with the success of his conquest.

Carol's resistance came to an end, and she covered her face with shame as he ripped off her dress. Frank's eyes burned as he stared at her. A fiendish laugh gurgled in his throat. He dragged her across the room. A hopeless despair settled on her.

Her bedroom door crashed open. Heavy footsteps rushed across the floor and a powerful hand jerked Frank Weaver to his feet. Carol looked up, unable to comprehend the miracle of her deliverance. Frank quivered with terror as strong fingers clutched his throat.

"Who's this weasel?" demanded Joe Mosley.

15   Deliverance

Within twenty-four hours after Joe rescued her from Frank, Carol's gratitude turned into aversion. Without waiting to be told anything, Joe had hit Frank so hard that he had broken his nose. Carol had no qualms about that, but the next morning when Joe learned that Weaver had been holding a bad check as a threat over her, he had left immediately for town. He returned that afternoon with the check.

"How did you get it away from him?" asked Carol in amazement.

"I told him to hand it over, or I'd break his nose again."

Carol's malicious glee at Frank's misfortune was short-lived. Joe's voice turned dark as he continued. "You didn't tell me it was a check of Monte Abbott's. I thought you had written it."

"You didn't give me a chance to explain."

"Why were you so damned anxious to protect him?" asked Joe suspiciously.

"He wrote it to help me out. I didn't want him to go to jail for that."

"And you were willing to give in to a fat slob like Weaver to protect Monte?"

"I wasn't giving in to him," Carol replied. "I had tried to get him drunk. Anyway, what business is it of yours?" asked Carol.

"You were plenty glad to see me."

"Sure I was, but I don't know why I have to answer to you for everything."

"Where is Abbott?"

"I don't know. He's been gone a week."

"If he wrote a check that got you into trouble, I'm going to see that he makes good on it."

"Let me have that check," Carol demanded.

"Nothing doing," said Joe, folding it into his pocket.

"But it doesn't belong to you. You can't collect on it."

"Why not? If a dope like Weaver can come close, I don't know why I can't go all the way," he smiled.

Carol felt as if she had gone from the frying pan into the fire. There was a vast difference, of course, between Joe Mosley and Frank Weaver. In times past, Joe didn't need to threaten her, but since she met Monte, she could not bear the thought of being in another man's arms.

"Just what do you think you're going to do?" she asked.

"There's been nothing but trouble since that Abbott showed up with his damn boat. I'm going to make sure he stays away," Joe replied.

"I'm running this dock, not you."

Joe glared then said, "It's about time you wake up, Carol. You've been playing around long enough, and it's gotten you into trouble. You need to get married. Settle down. You need a man to look after things for you."

"I suppose you mean yourself."

"I sure don't mean Monte Abbott."

"He's not the only one who ran out on me when things get rough. Don't forget you ran out when Bill Raft was trying to collect for repairs on his boat."

"I never owed it in the first place. And besides, I wouldn't have written a bad check. It's high time you and I got married and cut out this nonsense. You're a river girl and your dad would have been pleased to see me take over for you."

"I'm not planning on marrying anyone at the moment."

"You'll change your mind. I'm going into town for awhile. If Weaver gives you any more trouble, just let me know. If Monte shows up, tell him to beat it – quick. If he knows what's good for him."

"Is there anything else?" she asked sarcastically.

Joe left her seething. She was fed up with being pushed around – Hadley, Weaver, and now Joe. Monte let her down when she needed him most. Her world was closing in on her. She did not want to take this sort of treatment – she wanted to get away, start over somewhere. Nothing definitive came to mind, but she did resolve to take care of one thing. She needed to know where she stood with the Ebbs estate - either they would take over her business right now or stop harassing her. It was impossible to operate a business with a man like Weaver making her life hell.

At noon the next day, after Carol hurried through her work and took the bus into town. She arrived at the office where the Ebbs estate did its business, ready to demand Frank to put her in contact with the trustees. Frank was not there. In his place behind the desk sat a well dressed man with graying hair and a kindly look in his eyes.

"I came to see Weaver," she announced.

The man stood up behind his desk. "He met with an accident. I'm Conrad Ebbs. Is there anything I can do for you?"

"Yes, you're just the one I want to see," she said, introducing herself.

"Please sit down, Miss Burke. I've heard about you. But, of course, I've never had an occasion to meet you until now."

Carol sat down. She studied him a moment. "My dad made a loan with you people a long time ago. He paid on it, and then I've been paying on it since his death. Things aren't going too well at the Cabaret Dock. I'm doing the best I can. Weaver has been harassing me to constantly reduce the loan –"

"He has?" Ebb's eyebrows shot up. "I never told him to do that and I don't believe any other trustee did either."

"He threatened me with foreclosure time and again."

"Something's wrong there. I don't understand, but you certainly won't have trouble in the future. Just this morning I – "

"Did you know what Frank was doing?"

"I certainly did not, and I must say I'm shocked."

"You'd really be a lot more shocked if you knew what he was really after," she said.

"You mean our agent was bothering you, Miss Burke?" he gazed at her.

"Plenty –"

"I'll look into that right away, and you need not worry that the Ebbs Estate will ever be brought into it again. Just this morning I sold your mortgage."

Carole blinked, "But why?"

"A man got in touch with me late yesterday afternoon. He said he was interested in buying it. We do a good deal of trading of that kind, and we're especially interested in a cash deal because the trustees feel now is a good time to sell holdings."

Ebbs went on to explain that there had been a local promoter interested in purchasing Cabaret Dock and Island to make an amusement park. The promoter changed his mind because there were already two amusements parks in the area. The Chain of Rocks Park and the Forest Park Highlands were both losing business since Route 66 now by-passed the area. They were beginning to struggle just like Cabaret Clubhouse and Dock. The trustees on Carol's mortgage jumped at the chance to get some quick cash in order to buy more viable property.

Monte leaped into Carol's mind. A wild hope sprung up within her that somehow he had managed to straighten out his finances and, had decided to protect her and her business at the dock. Could it be that her luck had changed for the better at last?

"Abbott? Was that his name?" she asked quickly.

"No, it was a fellow by the name of Joe Mosley."

Carol was stunned. She knew Joe had a bank account. Most river men did. They were gone long stretches at a time on the river and they had less opportunity to spend money than men in other work. She did not dream, however, that he had saved that kind of money, enough to buy the mortgage on Cabaret Dock.

"Do you know him?" asked Ebbs.

"Yes," said Carol. "Quite well."

"Then I'm sure your mortgage is in good hands. You oughtn't to have trouble like you did with our Mr. Weaver. I wish right now to apologize for that, Miss Burke. And assure that Weaver will be dealt with."

"Did Joe – I mean Mr. Mosley, pay for it outright?" asked Carol.

"Yes, I happen to know he made a bank loan to cover the balance. He had well over half of it in cash of his own."

"Thank you."

Carol got shakily to her feet. Ebbs came around the desk and walked to the door with her. He was pleasant and wished her continued success at the dock. She remembered his words vaguely as she walked to the elevator and forgot them completely by the time she reached the street.

She began to understand what Joe had been talking about. He had said she would change her mind about him. He had talked as if her eventual marriage to him was a foregone conclusion. He had set himself up to force her to his way of thinking. Her only chance was to get out of business, let him take over. It was a bitter thought. Her dad had worked hard to get the Cabaret dock. If she walked out it would be like walking out on him.

On the other hand, she could not continue on without marrying Joe. She knew for sure that was why he had bought the mortgage. He would be crazy to buy it for any other reason. Carol walked along the street, so deep in thought, that she had no idea where she was going.

The pavements were hot, and downtown business moved at a slow pace. Stenographers, from cool, air-conditioned offices, hurried across the street to an air-conditioned restaurant for their afternoon coffee. Carol eyed them with envy. All they had to worry about were their nine-to-five jobs. In the evenings they could date the men they wished, free from the entanglements of business.

Carol not only had the worries that went with management, but the men who moved in on her because of it. She wished she was a stenographer, anything but what she was—a river girl. Still the river was all she knew. Anchors, deck cleats and boat hooks. Instinctively she walked toward the river.

A few minutes later she entered McTague's Tavern near the levee. She had not gone there for any particular reason, but she had wanted some place where she could sit down, cool off and think. When McTague asked what she wanted, she ordered a beer. She sat alone in a booth, smoking a cigarette. The beer was so refreshing that she had another one, and she was still sitting there at five o'clock when Joe Mosley came in.

"What are you doing here?" he asked, surprised.

"I had some business with Conrad Ebbs."

Joe sat down in the booth with her. He grinned across the table. "I guess he mentioned what happened this morning."

"You guessed it."

"We'll make that dock pay from now on, Carol."

"What do you mean by 'we'?"

"You and me, of course."

"Just because you own the mortgage is no sign you own the business—and you surely don't own me," she informed him sharply.

"Take it easy honey. Just relax, and you'll come around to my way of seeing this thing." Joe was trying to coax her into a better mood.

"Don't be too sure of that."

"We'll make a go of it. I'm not worried in the least. And the first thing we're going to do is tap your friend, Monte, for the thousand dollars he cheated us out of. I can collect on that check now, since it was meant for a payment anyway."

"You dare to bother him about that and I'll--"

"Bother? You're way behind me, Carol," he said. "I've already taken action."

"What have you done?" She felt appalled at his diabolical scheming.

"I made a few inquiries up and down the river to find out where he had gone with his boat. He's got it up at Grayson Dock on the Alton Lake under an assumed name. If he doesn't come through with cash for the check, the sheriff will snatch the boat and sell it."

"You've got a nerve, doing all that." Carol's lower lip quivered. "He was a customer of mine, not yours."

"Let's say ours now," Joe smiled.

She gave him a contemptuous glance, but she did not have time to argue. "Was Monte up at the dock with the boat?"

"No, the most I could find out was that he was in Cincinnati on business. But he'll come back—and when he does—" Joe paused and grinned. "I'll be waiting for him, if I haven't got action against him in the meantime."

Carol felt sick. Despite her mixed feeling toward Monte and the mess he had gotten himself into, she was worried about him. His predicament was as bad if not worse than hers. She felt a great yearning to help him, as he must have felt when he wrote that fatal check for her.

Joe was on duty that night. Otherwise, he said, he would go up to the dock with her. Carol said, "That's big-hearted of you. But it's a shame the *Della Darby* can't operate without your expert guidance."

Joe smiled at her sarcasm. "You'll get over that in time."

All the way back to the Cabaret Dock, Carol thought of nothing but the intolerable situations both she and Monte faced. She could see nothing ahead but catastrophe. With Monte a married man, she could see no possible solution to her hopeless love for him. There was one thing she could do, though, as a final gesture. She could inform him of the ill-will that had gathered in St. Louis to deprive him of his boat. It was probably the only possession he had left, and she knew he had sought to safeguard it by signing it under an assumed name at the Grayson Dock.

But how to get in touch with him? That stumped her. Cincinnati was a big place. She had not the faintest idea of how to begin searching for him there. Finally, after wracking her brain for a sensible solution, she went to the telephone and explained her problem to the long-distance operator. The operator was optimistic. Carol would be called back as soon as the call was put through.

She went outside, after changing into her dock uniform of halter top, shorts and yachting cap, straddled an oil drum and relaxed in the cool breeze that drifted across the river. The evening sky lost its brightness as the few clouds in the western heavens were tinted with pink and rose by the sinking sun. She looked at the great stream that flowed with deceptive gentleness at this time of year. Was she doomed always to a life on its high banks and muddy bosom?

Forty minutes later the ringing on the phone in the clubhouse interrupted her reverie. She went in, expecting a brief explanation of failure from the operator, and was astounded when she was greeted by Monte's voice.

"Monte," she exclaimed. "I didn't dream they would locate you."

"What's up? Any trouble?" he asked.

"Yes – lots of it." Her explanation was of necessity complicated. It involved Joe Mosley's plotting with regard to the mortgage, his interest in the whereabouts of Monte's boat, and the story about Monte's bad check. Monte had trouble understanding the unorthodox manner in which the check exchanged hands, but he had no trouble in understanding the jeopardy he faced in losing his boat when Carol mentioned that Hadley and her lawyer were also interested in its whereabouts.

"I thought you'd want to know all of that," Carol summed up.

"I should say so," he replied. Then contritely he said, "I was going to let you know where I am, Carol, but I've been awful busy with a lawyer here in Cincinnati. He thinks he has found a way to get me some relief. I'm coming back to St. Louis just as soon as I can."

"You'd better get back right away, if you don't want to lose your boat."

"It's impossible for me to get back right now." There was a moment of silence. "Carol, I wonder if you could get the boat and put it someplace where it wouldn't likely be found. Would that be asking too much, honey?"

His addition of that last single word of endearment was the adrenalin her heart needed. In a fraction of a second it changed her whole outlook. Before she even realized what she was doing, she agreed. A dozen unanswered questions flitted through her head but were held off by a long-distance proclamation of Monte's love.

Everything seemed suddenly so right when they finally hung up. It was not until quite a while later that she remembered Monte had registered in at the Grayson Dock under an assumed name. She made a frantic effort to get back in touch with him, but by then the operator reported that Mr. Abbott could not be reached.

16   Night of Terror

Retrieving Monte Abbott's cruiser and hiding it was no easy operation. Carol's failure to find out Monte's assumed name complicated matters at the Grayson Dock. She asked Matt to drive her there in the station wagon early the following evening, with instructions to return to Cabaret Dock and cross in the launch to the island where she would meet him sometime around midnight. She planned to anchor the cruiser in the slough at the same spot she and Monte had spent a glorious afternoon.

John Grayson, whom Carol knew well, was adamant when she told him she had come to take the cruiser away. "Its owner, a Mr. Pearson, had left no such instructions," he said. A dock operator was responsible for the safety of his customers' boats and did not let them be moved without orders.

"You know this fellow Pearson?" Grayson asked.

"Yes."

"Funny thing about him. Joe Mosley called here a few days back and described the same boat which he claimed belonged to a guy by the name of Abbott. He was surprised when I told him Pearson brought it in. What's this all about, Carol?"

"Nothing much, John," she said. "But he does want me to move the boat."

"Where to, Cabaret?" John Grayson and Carol were competitors indirectly. The main competition was between the lower Mississippi River and Alton Lake.

"Well, not exactly," said Carol, evading a direct answer.

"Tell you what I'm going to do," he said. "I'm going to put the responsibility for this squarely on you, Carol. If I hadn't known your dad so well and always respected you, I wouldn't think of letting a boat go out of here without instructions from the owner. You understand that?"

"Sure I do, John. I wouldn't be asking you to do something that was not legal."

"Okay, then. You can take it out. There's fifteen dollars due again here for docking fees. I suppose the owner told you to pay that," said John. He was not running his dock for his health.

Carol gulped. She had less than three dollars on her. "I'll send you a check in the morning."

"Well, okay," John replied.

Carol did not feel entirely safe until the lines were free and the engine picked up forward speed. Even then she did not feel too good about what she had done. She knew she had put a great amount of weight on her friendship with John Grayson. He could get into trouble if she did not hold to her responsibility. Monte's cruiser was worth at least ten thousand dollars.

That was a lot of money. She appreciated Monte's desire to keep it out of the hands of others. Joe Mosley could not do anything with it but tie it up in court. His estranged wife, Hadley and her lawyer, however, might be able to sell it and get the cash.

With the red and green running lights on, Carol stood at the wheel in the darkened deckhouse and headed down river toward the Alton Dam. She was lowered through the lock at ten-thirty and arrived just a little more than an hour later at the slough. She brought the cruiser in slowly, feeling her way to an anchorage with the spotlight. She went through the cruiser, making certain all was secure. Then she stripped naked and lowered herself over the stern by means of the small rope ladder. Holding her yachting cap, stuffed with her clothes, above the surface of the water, she swam around Cabaret Island on her back. She dried herself off the best she could, put on her shorts and halter top and walked down the beach in the moonlight to wait for Matt Davenport to pick her up in the launch.

From across the water she could see the light at the dock and a dim light on shore that Matt must have turned on in the clubhouse. The hooting of owls, crooking of frogs and buzzing of cicadas was a concert around her. She waited for what seemed an interminable time. It must now be long after midnight. She wondered why Matt did not come for her and kept watching for the navigation lights of the launch above the concert. Finally, the distant chug of the launch's motor came to her, and shortly afterward she made out the port and starboard lights as the launch came across the water. Everything had worked out fine.

As the launch approached the dock at the island, twenty minutes later, Carol stood ready to jump aboard. The engine was cut to slow speed. The spotlight came on, but to Carol's surprise it stabbed out in the wrong direction, probing the darkness for the dock.

"Hey, Matt?" she laughed as she called across the water.

The spotlight swung around instantly, as if startled by her voice. She stood in its glare, smiling at the old man. He had made the trip hundreds of times. Age was making him careless, or forgetful. Carol did not know which. The launch came on in, bumping against the dock with force. Carol stepped across. She chided him good naturedly.

"You handled the launch like you'd never been at the wheel before--" Carol stopped. Her heart leapt to her mouth. In the darkness she realized that this was not Matt at all. A squat figure left the wheel.

"That's not hard to understand," said Frank Weaver.

"What—are you doing here?" Carol gasped

"I came to get you. You wanted to be picked up."

"But—but where's Matt?"

"I left him back at the clubhouse."

Carol strained her eyes in the darkness, trying to see Frank's features and read the meaning of his words. Something was wrong. It was not like Matt to let a man who knew nothing about boats come after her in the launch at midnight.

"I thought it would be cozier that way," Frank added.

The tone of his voice sent a chill down Carol's spine. "You've got a nerve." she said, doing her best to keep the fear that she felt from creeping into her words.

"After what you did to me, that's all I have left. You got me fired. Conrad Ebbs gave me the pink slip this morning, and he told me why. You cheap little tramp. He told me about your visit to the office."

He stepped toward her and Carol retreated to the dock. She was not sure of her footing, and he caught her before she could go beyond his reach. Frank fastened his arms around her. Carol knew what she was in for. A blind unreasoning motive of revenge was added to Frank's passion. She struggled against him, and then cried out.

"Quit it, you fool. The launch. The launch—"

The running lights of the launch swayed gently in the water that had caught up with the boat's arrival. The space between the launch and the dock widened. Frank paid no attention to her at first, thinking she was merely trying to distract him. By the time he realized what was happening, the launch had floated to the rear of the dock and was sucked gently out into the current.

"Now look what you've done, you idiot," Carol raged.

Frank's first reaction was normal. He was embarrassed at his stupidity for not tying the boat down. He knew nothing of the river, and the slow receding lights of the launch were mute testimony to his inexperience.

"What'll we do?" he asked, turning to this river girl for advice. This made him uneasy, now that he had no way to return across the river to his familiar world.

"We're stranded here, until somebody picks us up. "

"How soon do you think that'll be?"

"Probably not until morning, unless we build a fire and attract attention. If Matt sees us, he'll come across in one of the customer's boats."

"No, I don't think he will," said Frank in a peculiar tone.

"He'll know something is wrong if he sees a fire over here at this hour," said Carol, who was preoccupied with the threatened loss of her launch to attach significance to his words. If she could signal Matt quickly enough, they might catch up with the launch and save it from destruction. She got down from the little pier and started across the sand.

"Where're you going?" asked Frank.

"I'm trying to find enough old papers and dry sticks to start a fire. The picnickers always leave a lot of stuff lying around."

There was just enough moonlight so that Frank could follow her as she moved a short distance up the beach. It occurred to her that she could return to Monte's cruiser, but that would give its presence away for one thing. For another it would invite further aggressive moves from Frank if he knew she held a means of escape. Furthermore, it would take as long to get the cruiser as it would to get Matt over here. If he came in a fast boat, they might yet save the launch.

"That won't do any good," said Frank, catching up with her.

"You're crazy. Get busy. Help me find something that will burn. You've got matches, I hope."

"But Matt won't see the fire," Frank observed in the same peculiar tone he used a moment ago.

This time its significance got through to Carol. She turned around and strained her eyes to see him better. An unaccountable apprehension came to her, "Why not?"

Frank was like a criminal whose time had run out. He had thought to return to Cabaret Dock, after he had finished with Carol, and somehow set things right with Matt. He had not killed the old man. He had expected to attend to him later, pay him off with a bribe or something so that he would keep his mouth shut about being knocked out. However, now that was out of the question. All of Frank's plans had gone hay-wire. All but one, which his evil mind was now considering. He began to feel doomed anyway. Before events caught up with him, he might as well go all the way.

"He just won't," Frank said smiling.

"What did you do to Matt back at the dock?" Carol began to understand now. She gasped, "You killed him."

"No. I'm not that bad. I just cooled him off for a while."

"You must be insane."

"If I am, it's because of you. Everything you've done to me. And what have I had to show for it? Nothing."

"Listen, Frank. For God's sake, come to your senses." She began to plead to his reason. "We can't stay here all night. You'll be in worse trouble than ever. We've got to get help."

"You're not going to light a fire," he said. Frank had little reason left.

"But—"

"You know what you're going to do," he grabbed her wrist. "And this time you're not going to get out of it."

Fear gripped her so tensely that for a second she could not move. She jerked away from him with all her might and started to run. Frank's hands reached out, but she eluded him. In doing so, she stumbled and fell to her knees. He rushed her, and for a wild, turbulent moment they rolled in the sand.

Carol was crazed with terror as he sought to encircle her with his fat, flabby arms. With a swift, instinctive move she clawed at the sand. His weight had about fastened her when she hurled the sand in his face. Frank sputtered with rage. With hysterical strength, she wiggled out of his grasp.

Frank caught her ankle, but she rolled and kicked so furiously that he could not hold on. She was up in a flash. Before Frank could get to his feet, she streaked off up the beach. He chased her, running with surprising speed for a heavy man. Carol's mind raced ahead of her flashing legs. She could never elude him on the beach all night.

She plunged into the cedar and willow thickets away from the beach. Frank roared after her. Sharp leaves cut at her flesh, and low-hanging branches clawed at her hair. She fought her way forward, panting with desperation. There was no moonlight in these black shadows, but Frank could hear. Carol banged into a river birch and almost knocked herself senseless. She staggered away. Her legs gave way - she fell. She dragged herself a few feet further and lay still as she felt an entanglement of bush honeysuckle at her back.

She heard Frank cursing and trashing through the underbrush. Her pounding heart and gasping breath would surely give her away as she lay like a cornered rabbit, hoping for the protection of the darkness. He stopped, and she could hear his labored breathing. Then he began beating the bushes for her again. He came so close that he almost stepped on her, and it was all she could do to stifle a cry of terror and agony.

His footsteps receded. Again he stood still. When he took up the pursuit, it was in a different direction. Carol had been holding her breath so long that her lungs were about to burst. She gave herself some air and let out a faint gasp. Frank paused and listened. He bent forward with renewed energy to get a sense of her direction, but by now he was confused in the darkness.

"Carol," he called. "Where are you? I won't hurt you."

His voice came to her from the direction of the beach. She knew he must have gone back there to get his bearings. She eased her position a bit and listened. Above the incessant croaking and buzzing she heard him break a stick attempting to probe for her in the sumac thickets.

Carol took this opportunity to put distance between them. Her sense of direction was about gone, too, and she looked up through the leaves for a familiar constellation. Matt had told her to rely on the Big Dipper if she was lost in the woods. She headed toward what she hoped was the northern tip of the island. If she could get there undetected, she might make it to Monte's cruiser. She would take it out of the slough if necessary. She was not going to spend the night on this island with a madman, if she could avoid it.

It was difficult for her to keep her balance, much less her direction in this blackness. She had taken several steps when her foot snapped a dried dogwood branch. It broke with a sharp crack. Frank ran along the beach and plunged into the undergrowth at the sound. Meanwhile, she stood stark still. In disgust he returned to the beach. She started on.

Carol never knew how long this game of dog-and-rabbit went on. Sometimes Frank would be far off from her. At other times, agonizingly close. It seemed to Carol that long dreary hours of pursuit had passed, and that she had progressed to the upper tip of the island. The last she had heard from Frank, he seemed many yards away. Out of breath, she crept to the edge of the undergrowth.

At first she could not believe where she was. She looked up and down the river, checking herself time and again with familiar lights. Instead of getting to the northern tip of the island, she had traveled south. She was almost back at the dock. She sank to her knees from disappointment and exhaustion.

Her mind glazed over. Minutes, maybe hours, went by. She did not know. In time, she heard the faint chug of a boat and could not process the strange formation of lights. Her dull mind tried to comprehend it.

It was several minutes later when a thought struck her as the boat and its strange lights seemed to be nearing Cabaret Dock. It was the Coast Guard. They had spotted the drifting launch and, knowing where it belonged, they were bringing it back up to the Cabaret Dock. *Thank you, Jesus.*

Her blood turned to ice. In her preoccupation with what was going on across the water, she had neglected Frank. A faint movement in the darkness of the beach attracted her attention. She stared and was able to see the vague outline of his hulking shadow. He was standing about ten feet away. He, too, had been attracted by the strange visit across the water at the Cabaret Dock. She froze and slowly squatted down behind a breached river birch, lowering her face and stilling her breath.

Carol knew if she made a move or a sound, he would look in her direction. If he looked, he most surely would see her. She knelt, stricken, fearful of breathing.

Meanwhile, the boat put in at Cabaret Dock. The river was far too wide for Carol to see what went on there, but she heard the distant engine cut to silence. She fought back a wild impulse to yell for help at the top of her lungs and hope that her screaming would somehow carry across the water. It would not, she knew. Best to conserve her strength for the ordeal ahead.

Frank moved. He had no idea what was going on across at the dock. He could only speculate on whether Matt had been discovered. His movement brought him even closer to Carol who almost sobbed aloud at this ill fortune. Her bent knees ached in such pain, that she did not think she could stand it a moment longer. She had been holding that same position forever.

Just what brought this impasse to an end, she never knew. Perhaps it was an unconscious movement on her part. Perhaps that sixth sense of someone near. In any event, Frank whirled around with a cry of astonishment. Carol gave a start and tried to rise. Her legs would not hold her. As Frank's hand fastened itself on her arm, she let out a shriek.

"Shut up," he said menacingly. He bent close to her as she lay sobbing on the sand. "What's going on over there?"

Carol was so worn out that she did not answer. He shook her viciously.

"Tell me. Who is that over there? Do you know?" His voice was heavy with fear. He was almost as fatigued as Carol.

"I don't know," she said weakly.

He sat up, holding her. Carol stared up, her eyes as tired and pale as the high stars. She was insensitive to pain now. Utter exhaustion had overtaken her. She closed her eyes. He continued looking across the water.

"I said answer me." Frank's sharp command came to her from a great distance. It grew more audible, and with it came a new pain. He was slapping her cheeks. "Why are they coming this way? Who is it?" His words were fraught with panic.

Carol was so far gone that she could not make her mind function. She did not know what he meant. She only knew that he leaped up and dragged her along the sand. This movement shocked her senses once more, and she let out another agonized cry for help.

She didn't try to think it through. She was sure the rock hit him in the forehead. He went straight down. Even while he slid into the river current, the back of his shirt puffing with air, his head bobbing like an apple, she couldn't stop screaming. In seconds the current took him under, and all she could hear was the incessant mumbling of the cool night wind. *Now, you've done it.*

A great, white eye seemed to stare at her for a few moments. Again she sank to the sand. She did not know where Frank was. She did not know anything, until she heard a strange voice.

"Careful, boys. Put this coat around her."

The next thing Carol knew she was sitting in the snug cabin of the Coast Guard's patrol boat. A cup of hot, black coffee restored life to her nerves. Her mind struggled back to reality. She looked up as the officer in charge held out a cigarette to her.

"What happened, Miss Burke? We caught your launch floating down river with no one aboard, and we took it back to the dock where we found Matt Davenport in a bad way. We knew something was wrong. Then one of the boys thought he heard a scream from the island," he said.

"Where's Frank?"

"Frank? Is that his name? Three of the boys dragged him from the river. We picked you and him up in the searchlight as we approached the island. You were on the beach. He was floating just past the dock."

Carol began to believe the miracle of her rescue. "What did he do to Matt?"

"The old boy is hurt pretty badly. We've sent him down to the Coast Guard sick bay. Two of the boys took him in your launch. What happened to him?"

"Frank beat him."

"Frank who?"

"Frank Weaver. He's been stalking me for weeks. I was across on the island waiting for Matt to pick me up. Instead Frank wrought Matt unconscious and came here instead of Matt. He tried, he— " she broke off in dismay.

"We know," said the kind officer. Then his voice turned grim. "The boys will have him aboard here in a few minutes. He just needed some medical attention and a head bandage."

Three husky Coast Guardsmen came aboard ten minutes later with Frank, who was mumbling incoherently. The patrol boat got under way, and headed back toward the Cabaret Dock. Carol looked out as they crossed the river. The eastern sky was growing light.

She had spent a night of terror on the island.

17 Safe at Home

The police came shortly after several Coast Guards and Carol were back to the clubhouse. They listened to Carol's story and tried to make sense out of what Frank said, but all they got from the sorry slob was gibberish. They hauled him away, charged with assault and battery as a beginner and said they would check with Carol later about additional charges. Two Coast Guards stayed stationed at the dock for the morning so that Carol could get some sleep without interruptions.

Carol woke at noon. She had come through a nightmare, but reality for the day swept to her with new activity. She had no idea how long it would take Matt to recover. Meanwhile, the dock was her lone responsibility.   She got dressed and left her room. To her surprise Joe Mosley was in the clubhouse, talking to Wally and the two men from the Coast Guard.

The servicemen informed her that her launch had been returned and that Matt was okay but would be laid up for at least a week. After they made certain she had recovered from the previous night's ordeal, they departed. Wally made her a breakfast, and Joe sat down with her while she ate.

"What's the real story, Carol?" he asked.

"There's only one story. If you talked to the Coast Guard, they probably told you what they knew."

"There's a lot they didn't know," said Joe. He added mysteriously, " and I didn't tell them,"

She glanced at him, "What didn't you tell them?"

"That you went to the Grayson Dock last night and got Abbott's cruiser."

"How did you find that out?" she demanded.

"All I had to do was call Grayson."

"What business is it of yours?"

"Yesterday a fellow by the name of Tom Griffin got in touch with me. Said he was Mrs. Abbott's lawyer. He had found out from Conrad Ebbs that I might know something, or I might be able to help them find out."

Carol let this information sink in. The conspiracy against Monte was gathering momentum. She eyed Joe closely. "And what did you tell him?"

"I didn't tell him anything, yet. Out of curiosity, I called Grayson just to see if the cruiser was still there. Imagine my surprise when he said you had taken it away."

"You've got a lot of nerve, sticking your nose into something that doesn't concern you."

"But this concerns me a lot. For one thing there's that check."

"You'll never use that against Monte," she flared.

Joe shrugged. "More important, I'm going to see to it that you don't get further involved with Abbott. He's no good."

"I suppose Griffin told you that."

"He didn't have to I already knew it. But I've got to admit Griffin didn't say any complimentary things about Abbott."

"You're helping them out, aren't you?" She accused. "You're on their side."

"I'm sure not on Abbott's side," he confided.

Carol had no trouble figuring that one out. Joe had learned from Griffin that Hadley was out to ruin Monte. That suited Joe just fine. He thought it would clear the way for his marriage to Carol. Abbott was the only remaining threat against him. With cruisin' Monte eliminated, Joe would completely dominate her.

"Then you're not on mine either," she said abruptly.

"We'll see about that later. Meanwhile, what did you do with the cruiser?"

"Don't you wish you knew?"

Carol finished her breakfast and went back to her desk. Joe remained at the table, deep in thought. Carol glanced through her mail. It was mostly bills. Several of them had reminders that they were past due. One letter contained a note from Mr. Cullen at the bank reminding her that her first payment on the thousand-dollar loan he had made should be paid the following week. Carol gave a blank stare at the papers before her.

She did not know what to do. Her financial affairs were in a hopeless mess. Now, on top of everything, Matt was sick and could not help her at the dock. She felt as if the world was caving in on her. As she contemplated her troubles she saw Joe go to the phone booth. He talked to someone for five minutes, then came out smiling.

"Anything I can be doing for you around the dock?" he asked. "You'll need some help with Matt out of the picture for a while."

"I don't need your kind of help," she told him.

Joe came back and rubbed Carol's brunette head playfully. "Snap out of it baby, you've gotten yourself all mixed up. I'll help you around the dock. I've got a lot of interest in this place now."

"Let me alone."

"I'll pull the launcher in for you," he volunteered. "There's been some bad weather in the upper Missouri in the past two days. The river is on the rise."

"What are you so happy about all of a sudden? Who did you call just now?" she asked suspiciously.

"Some friends of yours. They're coming out for a visit this afternoon."

"Who?"

"Oh, you'll see." With that Joe walked out of the clubhouse and went to work, taking up the slack in the dock lines.

Carol knew Joe had something big to spring on her, but was not going to give him the satisfaction of begging for information. She kept a wary eye on him as she went about her work. She trusted him with the launcher and other odd jobs around the dock. Joe was a river man. He knew his business when it came to that. And he had been right about what one glance at the dock's gauge told her - the river was rising.

She thought of Monte's cruiser. If the river came up much higher, the *Carol* would have to be attended to. It might come free and drift against the shore or be carried out in the current, but there was no chance of getting to it with Joe around. She would have to wait until nightfall to take care of that. The river would not come up so fast that she could not wait until then.

Later in the afternoon, as Carol came out of the boatshed to check her supply of grease, she saw a car that had just pull up in front of the clubhouse. Not far away stood Joe, talking to a man and a woman. Carol started for the clubhouse. It was then that she recognized Hadley and Griffin

"There she is now," said Joe, motioning toward her.

Carol went on into the clubhouse, her head high. She did not care to speak to either of them, but she had no choice in the matter. They followed her in.

Griffin acted as spokesman. "Miss Burke, we've learned that you removed Abbott's cruiser from its dock on the Alton Lake last night."

Carol glared at Joe " – you dirty snitch. You told them."

"All I told them was what they could've found out by calling Grayson. I don't know where the cruiser is."

"What did you do with it?" asked Griffin.

"Sank it," Carol snapped.

"We wouldn't be asking for this information if it wasn't important, Miss Burke. Please-"

"What's so important about it? The boat doesn't belong to you."

"My client has a claim against it," Griffin smiled at Hadley. Carol glared back at the girl, "Well, isn't that just too bad?"

"Miss Burke, you took the boat," Griffin went on, ignoring her. "You're tampering with justice. It doesn't belong to you, either. I might add that you're getting yourself in to some trouble by keeping its whereabouts a secret. It could even be that you have stolen the boat."

"I did not. Monte asked me to move it."

"Oh, he did. Hadley cried. "Well, Tom, doesn't that prove she's his accomplice? Doesn't that put them both in the soup?"

Carol was startled by this outburst. She sensed that she had been trapped into giving information she should have kept to herself. Then Griffin spoke up. It does, indeed, Hadley. But that's secondary at this point. The most important thing is to locate the boat.

"Can't we have her arrested or something?" Hadley demanded.

Griffin smirked. He knew the bitter hatred that existed between the women. "Perhaps we could, but let's keep our eyes on the ball. Let's locate the boat first."

"You can't have me arrested. I haven't done anything," Carol challenged.

"Let me put it this way," Griffin said suavely. "You tell us where the boat is, and we'll give a second look at how guilty we think you are."

"Guilty of what?"

"Theft and conspiracy."

Carol knew nothing about legal matters but her native shrewdness told her that she had done nothing wrong or illegal. She suspected Griffin of trying to bluff her. She knew why Hadley wanted the cruiser. The sleek blonde had ten thousand dollars worth of reasons.

"I don't believe you," Carol flung back.

"Come on, Tom, let's not waste our time with her another minute. Let's get the sheriff," said Hadley.

"Why don't you come to your senses, Carol?" Joe spoke up. "These folks know what they're doing. They're not fooling. Griffin's a lawyer. Your just getting yourself in deeper by holding out on them. What's Abbott ever done for you that you should risk an arrest for his sake."

Carol answered that question with stone silence. All Monte had done was to take her heart. If she could go along with her reason, she would not be standing here, defying the three of them. She wanted to believe in Monte. Here entire judgment was influenced on a slender instinctive belief in him.

"Don't forget, he's still married," Joe added.

That remark only increased Carol's determination, but outwardly only. Inside it made her sick with indecision. Sure, Monte was married. He had caused her nothing but trouble and heartbreak. She saw no way out, no chance of happiness with him. All she had to go on now her heart.

"You have absolutely nothing to gain by your stubbornness, Miss Burke, and a great deal to lose," said Griffin. "We're going to locate that boat somehow, even if we have to resort to having you arrested."

"Go ahead. Have me arrested," Carol cried. Her nerves were beginning to show. She had been through so much that arrest did not frighten her. It would be a relief to be some place where people could not get at her to make her life more miserable.

"You aren't being been very sensible," Griffin reminded her.

"How can I be, with everyone trying to push me around?" Carol cried, almost in tears.

"All the more reason you should give us the info we're after. We'll get out and let you alone," the lawyer went on, sensing her emotional conflict. "There's no use in your suffering just to save Monte Abbott for a little while longer. He can't possibly save that boat."

"Aw, go on, Carol. Tell them and get it over with," Joe said.

"We'll leave the moment you tell us," Griffin assured her.

Carol averted her eyes. Anguish and dismay crossed her face. Even if she told them, they could get the boat. Joe or somebody would have to go after it for them. She wished Monte had never asked her to help him with it. He had placed her in an intolerable position. That had not been very considerate of him.

"Where is it, Miss Burke?" Griffin asked gently. The pressure of the moment drove Carol almost to the end of her endurance. She looked tired and fatigued. *Why not tell them? What the hell?*

The telephone rang. She walked to the booth. It was probably another one of her creditors asking for some money. She was right.

"Carol," said John Grayson. "I just want to check and make sure that you put my money in the mail."

"Oh – John, I haven't but I will right away."

"I'll be expecting it in the first delivery in the morning."

"You'll get it," she said and hung up. She went out of the booth.

"Another reason it won't do any good to hold out, Carol, is that I can just about tell where that boat is," said Joe.

"Well , why don't you then?"

"I'd have to look around a bit to make sure, but if you brought it down river there are only a few places you could have tied it up where it's be safe."

"Then if you know so much, why don't you help them out?" Carol spoke for her own morale by now. What Joe said was true. Anyone who knew the area could locate the cruiser in a short while. If it was hidden below the Alton Dam, it had to be in this vicinity. She had not been gone long enough to take it far.

"You see Miss Burke, this whole thing is absurd. Won't you tell us and get it over with?" Griffin asked. She hesitated. Her mind was considering when the phone rang again. With a sigh she went to answer it. The moment she heard the voice at the other end she closed the door to the booth.

"Monte. Where are you?" she gasped into the phone.

"Out at the airport. I just got in."

She moaned with relief. Then she gave him a quick summary of what was going on at the clubhouse. Monte listened in silence. Then he said, "Don't tell them, Carol. Please don't. Everything is going to work out all right."

"How, Monte, how do you know?"

"Because I'm right and they're wrong."

It was not the answer she wanted. Not quite at any rate. She needed complete assurance. "Don't you know for sure?" she pressed.

"Yes, honey. I know for sure, but there are a couple of missing details."

"Nothing can wait, Monte. They've threatened to have me arrested."

"That's ridiculous."

"Then why don't you come here right away?"

"I don't want them to know I'm in town, not yet. There is one little matter that must be attended to in the morning. I've arranged for it. Please, hold them off, Carol. I'll come out tonight."

"You can't. Joe is here. He'll cause you trouble."

"Could you meet me at the boat later. Where is it?"

"You remember where we went swimming at the head of the island that day? It's in the slough, anchored a short distance from shore."

"I guess I could hire that fellow Rafferty to run me up there late tonight. Could you come over in the launch? I'll explain everything. Might even have something more definite to report to you."

"I—I suppose I could."

"I love you, Carol. See you tonight," he said and hung up.

Carol walked out of the phone booth. Dillon stepped up to her. He gave her a smile. "You were about to tell us the location of the boat," he said. He looked at her with expectation.

Carol eyed him. Her gaze traveled on to Joe, who sat on a stool at the counter, a cigarette hanging from his lips and a half-smile curling their corners. She looked at Hadley. The girl regarded her with a haughty contempt, as if Carol could no longer defy them.

"I've changed my mind," said Carol. "Now get the hell out of here!"

18   Where's the cruiser?

"Of all the stupid things I ever heard of, that takes the cake," Joe ranted and raved after Hadley and Dillon had departed. "Now they'll go get the sheriff and come back here with a warrant for your arrest."

"If you knew so damned much, why didn't you tell them where the boat is?" she shot back.

"I know it's somewhere between here and the Alton lock. Any idiot would know that. And I'll find it for them, too, first thing in the morning. If you haven't got enough sense to keep out of jail, maybe I can get them to call if off by finding the boat for them."

"You want them to have it instead of Monte. You're more interested in that than you are in keeping me out of jail."

Joe smiled, "No, it doesn't exactly suit me to have you locked up. I've got plans for you and me, baby."

Carol went out. It she talked to Joe one more minute she would explode. She escaped to the dock and put gasoline into the launch. She wanted to make sure she would have enough for her trip to the head of the island tonight. She did a couple of other chores while she was there. As she mounted the steps, half an hour later, she saw a dark line of clouds, low in the southwest. It would get dark early tonight and that suited her fine.

A rain crow took off from the top of one of the elms as she entered the clubhouse. The air was growing oppressive and still. Carol knew what that dark line of clouds meant. She hoped the rain would hold off until she could keep her rendezvous with Monte. Joe was seated at the counter with a bottle of whiskey and beer nearby when she came in.

"Have a drink," he offered.

"No thanks."

It was Wally's night off, so Carol fixed herself a sandwich and made a pot of coffee. Joe helped himself to some food but went right on drinking. She glanced at him.

"What time do you have to be at work tonight?" she asked.

"No time. I told them to get another skipper for the 'Della Darby'. From now on I'm looking after my investment in the Cabaret Dock."

"You're not going to sleep here," said Carol.

"Can't think of a better place."

She could not have that, not with Monte in the vicinity. "Listen to me, Joe. You've taken an awful lot for granted lately. You were a fool to buy the mortgage on this place. Just because you did is no sign I'm going to knuckle under to your whims."

"You're the one who's been a fool. You've gotten big ideas about this guy, Monte. You thought you'd get him away from his wife. You thought you'd leave the river, go high society. Well, let me tell you something. Monte's a phony, and you're just a river girl, and you'll never be anything else. I'm taking my time from now on to straighten you out."

A white ridge of anger showed along her jaw line. For days and weeks, she had been headed off, frustrated at every turn. Her creditors, Frank Weaver and the others, Hadley and her lawyer, and even to some extent, Monte. All had unsettled the course of her life and her instincts. Like the great river that had been her home, she had been held against her will, between man-made levees and dikes and artificial channels. All at once she was incensed with rebellion.

Words flooded to the surface, broke over the levees, like the river on a rampage. Her vocabulary, learned since childhood from engine rooms, pilot houses and river front establishments, was spicy. She inundated Joe with a torrent of profanity that caused him to marvel in respectful silence.

"And now, by God, if you don't get out of here," she raged, "I'm going to lay your head open with that bottle."

She had grabbed the neck of Joe's whiskey bottle as she talked, and now brandished it at him as a threat. Joe's eyes were bright with admiration. This was a turn on for him. It was the kind of talk he understood.

"After hearing that, I'm beginning to think there's some hope for you". He smiled. "You sounded more like yourself just now than you have in a long, long time, Carol."

"Are you going to get out?"

"Damned if I don't think I will. I'm not nearly as worried about you now as I was five minutes ago. Mind if I take my bottle with me?"

She set it back on the counter. The moment she let go of it, he grabbed her. He chuckled as her fist punched off his jaw. He pinned her arms to her sides and laughed with excitement as she struggled. Surprisingly, he let her go after he had forced his lips on hers. The tongue-lashing she gave him was responsible for that. Carol spoke Joe's language.

"Here's to us, baby," he said. Uncorking the bottle, he took a deep swig and then walked to the door, "See you later."

Carol went to her room. As she calmed down, she was satisfied to have gained a point through her sheer will power. She had gotten rid of Joe for the night.

Next, she turned down the lights in the clubhouse to discourage anyone from coming over from Riverview Drive. With Matt gone, she did not want any visitors loitering around while she was gone.

At nine o'clock she went down to the dock. There was lightning in the west. With a storm coming up, it meant she would have to get back to the dock before it broke. Someone had to be here in case of an emergency. She prayed that Monte had reached his cruiser by this time.

She cast off the lines mooring the launch, started the motor in the darkness of the cabin and headed up the river. When she was safely underway, she glanced toward the west. The storm was still quite a way off. It would not break in this vicinity until around midnight. Two miles north of Cabaret, she altered her course and crossed the river.

As she neared the northern-most point of the island, she throttled to slow speed. She was out of the channel and had to be careful, lest she go aground on a sandbar. She put on the spotlight and began feeling her way around the north point. She would need it later to pick up the cruiser in the darkness. As the launch came around into the slough, she was startled to see the cruiser lighted from bow to stern.

At the sound of the launch's motor, Monte came on deck and waved to her. For one delicious moment she let herself thrill at the sight of him. Then she got control of her emotions. She had done everything she could for him. The future was up to him. Unless he had some definite plan to suggest, Carol knew they would be lost to each other forever.

She brought the launch around and eased it slowly up against the cruiser. Monte took the line she tossed him and tied it promptly. With a cry of happiness, he reached across and held her hand as she stepped over into his boat.

She gave in to the delight of his embrace for a minute, then pushed him away. She looked at him. His eyes seemed worn out, but there was a smile of happiness on his lips.

"I've got so much to tell you that I don't know where to begin," he said.

"You might begin by explaining why you've got all the lights on. That isn't a very good way to keep the boat's location a secret."

"That's not important any longer, but I guess you're right. It'll be more fun holding you in the darkness."

He turned off all but the port and starboard running light. In the darkness the lightning in the west appeared exaggerated. Carol noticed that the storm was approaching faster than she had expected.

"I can't stay here long, Monte. There's no one back at the dock. I've got to be there if there's going to be much wind and lightning tonight."

"It was sure considerate of you to come over, and it was thoughtful of you, too, to take the time to bring my boat down from Alton Lake."

"Hadley and her lawyer say they're going to have me arrested for it."

"Nonsense! Let them try."

Again he folded his arms around Carol. She felt his heart pounding against her. Carol's pulse quickened. Her heart ruled her head when it came to Monte. She had come here to get information, yet, now all she wanted was the tenderness of his lips, warm and exciting against hers.

"Please Monte, we've got so much to talk about and I have to hurry back," she said , breaking away from him.

At that instant there was a sound of movement in Carol's launch. Both Monte and she cast a glance in that direction. Carol thought she was seeing an apparition. A shadowy figure stood up in the stern of the launch. The next second it leaped aboard the cruiser. Carol let out a muffled cry.

"Who in the hell?" Monte breathed.

He turned on the cruiser's lights. There in the cockpit stood Joe, his face as stormy as the towering thunderheads bearing down from the west.

"How did you get here?" she gasped.

"You didn't think I was really going to leave you alone at the dock, so I came down to sleep on the launch. I heard you come down and start up. I figured you were coming to meet this bastard somewhere, so I just lay quiet and waited to see what all would happen."

"Now that you know," Monte said. "Get off my boat."

"You'll play hell making me do anything from now on, Abbott. A lot of people have been looking for you, me included. You've got a lot of answering to do for a trail of bad checks you left behind, and I think your wife and her lawyer have got a few surprises for you too."

"Monte, no!" Carol screamed as he lunged forward.

Monte was blind with fury. He charged toward Joe who swung his right hand out in a lightning-like move from behind his back. In his fist was the wrench from the engine box on the launch. Monte was so enraged that he did not see the weapon. As he aimed a blow at Joe's jaw, the wrench swung around and caught Monte on the temple. He was knelt down on the deck cushion.

Carol ran to him. After a single groan, he went limp. She shook him in a rage of fear. Her eyes were wild and pleading as she looked up at Joe.

"You've killed him," she screamed.

I hope so, Joe stepped back. He lost interest in Monte. He too could see the signs of the approaching storm and knew what it meant.

Joe went to work in quick and efficient fashion, to get the launch at the stern of the cruiser and secure it with two lines. With that accomplished, he paused to look down at Carol , who was still bent over Monte. "We're starting back," he said.

"I'm not leaving Monte here in this condition."

Joe grunted. "Nobody said we were. I'm taking him and his damned cruiser back. They're both going to be where people can find them in the morning. We'll tow the launch behind."

"No, you're not moving this cruiser."

"You're not giving me orders any longer. I'm the guy who's doing that. "

Joe entered the deckhouse and started the motor. He turned off the lights and ordered Carol to bring the boat forward while he lifted the anchor. Dumbstruck, she obeyed. Her mind was in a panic over Monte who had not moved since the wrench slammed his head.

With instinct she responded to handle the boat properly. As Joe pulled up the anchor, she saw the menacing streaks of lightning across the river. The storm was too close for comfort. There was no time to argue with Joe about leaving the cruiser here. For its own safety, it had to be taken to shelter of the dock along with the launch. That went for safety of all three who were aboard too.

When Joe called that the anchor was clear, she headed the cruiser out of the marsh at full speed. Joe came back and stood by her at the wheel. Both knew the danger of the sandbars, and their eyes probed the darkness for markers. In a few minutes, they were in safe water and headed for the channel.

The lightning showed the cumulus clouds in the night sky and thunder boomed almost overhead. During this time, neither Joe nor Carol spoke. Their minds were those of river people, focused with the intimidation of storm and current.

Once they were beyond an underwater sandbank, however, during one flash of lightning, Joe stared at Carol's bare legs and her firm, young figure, superbly outlined by a T-shirt and tight-fitting slacks. After the liquor he had drunk earlier in that evening, his success in doing in his rival and the approaching excitement of the storm, Joe was keyed up.

He stood in back of her and put his hands on her waist. "My girl," he muttered.

"Get the hell away from me," she jerked away. "I'm steering the boat and launch down the river to safety.

"Want me to take the wheel?" Joe asked.

His words were drowned in a great explosion of thunder. It was followed by another burst of lightning. The surface of the river stirred under a rushing gust of wind. In that flash of light, she saw the gray wall of rain advancing toward them like a tornado's curtain.

Seconds later, the storm broke. With a wild howl, the wind engulfed them and drove tons of water down the river and the boat. Chopping waves lashed at the river, and the cruiser began to rock. The rain was so heavy that even during explosions of lightning, the trailing launch was obscured from their view. They were in the choke hold of a raging river and squalling storm, with no chance of sighting blinkers, the chain of rocks or familiar landmarks on shore.

Carol glanced back over her shoulder. Just then a flash of lightning revealed Monte standing in the door of the deckhouse, blood streaming down his cheek. The cold and pounding rain revived him. Joe saw him, too.

Next, the cabin was plunged into darkness. Over the roar, Carol heard the two men shouting challenges and defiance at each other. They struck blows at each other.

Carol groaned with a final despair. The two men were at each other's throats, and one would surely not survive the fierce hatred that flared between them. She knew she did not dare leave the wheel of the tumbling cruiser, lest all three of them be swallowed up by the yellow giant river.

19   The Finale

In the blackness of the deckhouse and howling storm, the two men grappled with savage fury. It was not enough that nature's elements sought to tear the boat apart; two humans inside flung themselves against its interior walls with such force, Carol expected the cruiser to fly apart at any moment.

She screamed over the wind, but neither man heard her. One part of her mind tried to navigate the boat, and other tried to halt the pandemonium. For a while she experienced fear as the lightning, gradually abating, showed her the two men straining against each other for their lives. The combat shifted to the cockpit, and in a final spark of lightning Carol saw a fist clubbing down on one of the fallen men. She did not know which one.

She functioned by instinct now. There was no trace of the shore through the driving slant of the rain. She had no idea where they were. Without knowing why, she turned the water craft around, felt the jerk of the launch on its towline, and began edging in toward Missouri's bank. To her amazement a bobbing light on the dock appeared dimly through the deluge. She let the boat fall back with the current, then went in even closer to the bank and up under the protecting arbor formed by the dock floats.

The protection was minor at best. The dock itself was buffeted by the wind and water; its planks creaked and groaned as the river heaved and surged. As if in a nightmare, Carol brought the cruiser into a slip. She made a dangerous leap from its bow with a line and almost had her wind knocked out of her as the dock came up to meet her. Somehow, she got the line tied to a metal cleat.

She crawled on her hands and knees along the catwalk of the slip and pulled the launch into the slip beside the cruiser. In an agony of dread, she went back aboard the cruiser and turned on the lights. Monte was lying against the sopping wet cushions of the cockpit, his hand crossing his eyes in an attempt to clear his head. Joe was stretched out on the deck, limp and unconscious.

Carol started toward Monte then collapsed.

The next morning, Carol awakened in her own bed. Daylight flooded her room. She looked out and saw the river, again quiet and serene, flowing south on its way to the Gulf. A tide of hysterical memories from last night quickened her movements as she hurried into her clothes and ran out of the clubhouse.

Her fear and panic mounted as she rushed down the steps to the dock, and along its planks to Monte's cruiser. She dreaded the grisly sight that she knew was there. A stranger arose from a deck chair as she approached. She stared at the man.

He looked at her with curiosity, then asked, "Are you Miss Burke?"

"Yes."

"Glad to know you. My name is Crawford."

Just then Monte came out of the deckhouse. His eyes looked blood shot and his face was gaunt from the strain of last night. He smiled when he saw Carol.

"Come on aboard," Monte urged her. "I was just making some coffee and want you to meet Jack Crawford."

Crawford acknowledged the introduction as she stepped over onto the cruiser. Carol was so surprised that she could say nothing. She had expected an entirely different scene to greet her.

"Where's Joe," she asked.

"After the storm quieted down last night, I called the police over here. They helped me get you to your room and took Joe to a hospital. He's probably come around by now and oughtn't to suffer anything more serious than a broken arm and a hangover."

"You folks were lucky to get in off the river alive," said Crawford. "Monte told me about the storm on the Mississippi River last night. It was the same type of squalling storm that caused your mother's death in 1936."

"Wait a minute. What do you know about my mother's death?"

Carol sat down. Crawford smiled and with friendly eyes, looked at her. "Monte has the craziest way of getting himself involved with financial matters. He said you knew a little something about it, but he can explain more about your mother later. I'm his lawyer from Cincinnati. I came to help the situation and make sure he keeps his employment with the federal government for special assignments."

"Oh?" She waited for him to go on.

"We've got it pretty well cleared up. There were legal shenanigans pulled against Monte that were largely bluff. My advice to Monte going forward is to keep his affairs close to his belt. Maybe look after them a little more and this cruiser a little less."

Monte turned to her. "I'm solvent again. That damned crooked lawyer Griffin had almost coerced me into giving over everything I own. They've got no claim against me at all for monthly alimony. They couldn't even attach this boat."

Carol did not say anything. She was glad it had worked for him, but nothing changed much for her.

Monte and Crawford talked on as they drank their coffee. When they finished Monte said, "I don't want to hurry you, Jack, but I'd appreciate it if you'd get over to the hospital and talk to that fellow Joe Mosely. You might also check to see if Griffin got away."

Carol had no idea what he was talking about. Right now she did not care to inquire. After what she had been through, she was content to sit here on the stern of this comfortable cruiser and drink her coffee. Crawford left a few minutes later.

"Well, that ought to about do it," Monte remarked.

"Do what?"

"Jack went right to work with Hadley and her lawyer when we got in. He came over with me from Cincinnati. Last night and this morning he convinced them of the facts of life. He told Hadley either to make a settlement, or he'd get a divorce filed for me. She's been running around with Dillon Griffin, and I've got plenty of grounds for fraud against my checking account.

Carol stared. "She-she's going too?"

"Hadley took the settlement, and right now she's bound for Reno."

Carol was stunned. Monte moved close to her and slipped his arm around her waist. He brushed her cheek with a kiss.

"If you'll have me," he said, "I want to marry you, soon as we can."

A powerful shot of hope jolted to her heart and had to steady herself in disbelief. Her large luminous eyes began to shine, a smile appeared – timid at first and then on her lips. She flung her arms around him. At that moment, she heard footsteps and Matt appeared on the deck. "My, my what have we here ?"

For a blissful moment she knew the ecstasy of a joy she had never dreamed possible. Then, she pushed back.

"But what's this with Joe? Why does Mr. Crawford want to see him?"

"Oh, I forgot to tell you. Jack looked up the mortgage on this place. Turns out that since your mother was a descendant of the Iroquois Nation, due to her death in waters near Cabaret Island in a storm, unless the United States Federal Government lays a claim within ten years, known as the Guano Islands Act of 1890, she and her descendants own the island. Next, I'm buying the mortgage on the Cabaret Clubhouse and Dock and giving Mosley that bad check as his profit. The Carbaret is going to belong to us, Carol."

"We own Cabaret Island, Cabaret Clubhouse and Dock. It's all ours."

She was too surprised and overcome with happiness to say anything just then. A film of tears blurred her eyes. Monte went on.

"I was thinking of expanding to a second location near Alton Lake. We can start all over. I'll love helping you and Matt run a dock. I always wanted to be a river man."

Epilogue: Matt's Story

The next afternoon, Matt Davenport was brought back home to the Cabaret Clubhouse in the launch. Carol greeted him at the dock with a great big hug. She insisted that he come inside and made him as comfortable as possible in the rickety captain-style office chair. He was embarrassed for all the attention but did accept the cup of coffee that was pressed into his hand.

"Cap't, I'm sorry I let that guy Frank get the best of me. I had no idea you were in such danger. How long has this been going on?"

"I'm fine, Matt. Really. It wasn't your fault."

"It's time, heck, it's long past time. Your father, Sam, asked me to take care of you and give you your birthright when you were ready. The strongbox on the shelf behind the desk. Look inside for a secret compartment at the very bottom. There are three documents he wanted you to have. One is your mother's birth certificate and the second is your parents' marriage license. It's a long story that you should know. The third document is an American Indian tribal certificate. Sam Burke just couldn't talk about it with you."

Matt settled in as Carol clutched the yellowed papers and Matt told his story. It went on till the shadows of an early evening slowly paraded across the room.

It seems that back in the summer of 1932, the boat that Sam Burke was piloting put in at La Crosse, Wisconsin. On the way back down the Mississippi River, the cook had quit and they needed a replacement for the return trip. A beautiful, young woman named Ima Jean Windsong showed up to take the job and soon had everyone on the boat including Matt falling in love with her.

It was Sam Burke who stole her heart and they were married by the time they got back to Cairo, Illinois. Ima Windsong's family was a descendant of the Iroquois Nation, sometimes called the Six Nations. Her tribe was the Seneca tribe, settled in Wisconsin following their Peace Treaty in 1838.

Ima Windsong loved her family but had wanted to change her life and see the world. She and Sam lived together on the boat. After Carol was born, she was left with Sam's relative in Cairo, whenever Sam and Ima traveled on the Mighty Mississippi. One dreadful night in 1936 a storm ravaged the chain of rocks area in the Mississippi River and Ima was thrown overboard, near the tip of Cabaret Island. Indian legend says after she passed from this world. Matt said, "Sam cherished her Manitou stone talisman where her spirit remains and she has guided you." Carol responded, "I never questioned its positive energy and spirit of my mother, and will wear it on a necklace."

"It holds the memory of Ima's dream that her daughter would remain near Cabaret Island, using her rightful ownership as an Iroquois descendant."

Cast of Characters

Carol Burke

Monte Abbott

Matt Davenport

Hadley Abbott

Frank Weaver

Judy Lewin is an author, researcher and forensic genealogist living in St. Louis, Missouri with her husband, Steve and beagle, Roxie. Judy is a member of the St. Louis Writer's Guild, St. Louis Publisher's Association, St. Louis Genealogy Society, National Genealogical Society and Romance Writers of America. She has won several writing awards including first place in Writers Type Contest, October, 2013; Private Investigator For Hire Genealogist small business achievement award for St. Louis City, 2013; and a **Brag Medallion** awarded by Independent Publishers Association, 2014. *Body-Slam Diva:* Dancer becomes Champion Wrestler, 2014.

Visit her website at www.JudyLewin.net

Please email her at JudyLewin@msn.com

Thank you.

www.ingramcontent.com/pod-product-compliance
Lightning Source LLC
Chambersburg PA
CBHW021048130626
46552CB00005B/2070